The Silence of the Glasshouse

MARTIN MALONE

NEW
ISLAND

The Silence of the Glasshouse
First published 2008
by New Island
2 Brookside
Dundrum Road
Dublin 14

www.newisland.ie

ISBN 978-1-84840-001-6

British Library Cataloguing Data. A CIP catalogue record for this book is available
from the British Library.

Book design by Inka Hagen.
Printed in Denmark by Nørhaven Paperback A/S

New Island received financial assistance from
The Arts Council (An Chomhairle Ealaíon), Dublin, Ireland.

10 9 8 7 6 5 4 3 2 1

For Mam and Dad

Prologue

10 February 1922, 11:00 hours

Every Friday morning he walks to the Hibernian Bank on the main street to collect the pay for his men in the Royal Field Artillery Barracks. As a military man from a family steeped in a long military tradition, he loves routine and order. Discipline, too. These traits are bred in him, as are his slender frame and strong physique. A touch of stubbornness about his chin, a glint of humour in his eyes, a brush of defiance in his gait, and owning too that certain recklessness of the young, that phase of youth when tender years often fool a man into believing that he is invincible, that immortality is not beyond him. A vibrant soul in his confident air, his precise and clipped diction, words pushed from the corner of his mouth, thoroughly developed before birthing. He is aware of where he has come from and knows where he wants to go in his life. His friends, of whom he has many, agree on one point: he is a stickler for adhering to rules and regulations, and never once relaxes them for fear that such lapses might be construed by others as a sign of weakness and by himself as something he might overindulge in if he is not on his guard – laxity, diffidence. Failings of his uncles, whose lack of attention to detail had cost them their merchant business.

His thoughts in the bank centre on the last game of the rugby season, when he had gone over on his ankle and how if he had managed to avoid the injury he would have been in fine fettle for the coming athletic meets. Last June he had finished second in a first-class half-mile to a guest black runner from Jamaica, beaten by the width of his singlet – there won't be a Jamaican flier in the line-up this year. Depends on the ankle, sore, sore, sore. Bags of ice and running cold water, restricted to light walking … the enforced inactivity frustrates and irritates him.

Pretty thing behind the counter. Nice face, pleasant.

The cashier counts out £135 in notes and coins and he puts it in his canvas bag, says, 'Thank you,' and leaves.

She is disappointed that he had not said anything else to her. He seems shy and preoccupied. His name is John Wogan Browne. Last week she had heard the manager say that he came from one of the oldest and most respected Roman Catholic families in the county. Distinguished, he'd breathed. Like he had a craving in him to be as highly regarded.

Outside the bank, he turns right and walks along the path, passing the redbrick post office and across from it, the courthouse.

Now, he thinks, *if I can have the men paid by dinner-time, I'll take a motor in the afternoon and perhaps visit Jerry in*

Newbridge. He said he might have word on the date of the battery's return to England. He knows everyone, that lad – ingratiating fellow.

The street is empty of people.

A few yards ahead of him, parked outside the gates of the convent school, he sees a Model-T Ford, the hood raised. Instantly, he grows suspicious – it's a mild sort of day, not a threat of rain. Concerned, he looks behind him, thinking it might be prudent to return to the bank and summon help, but he sees a man with hands buried in his pockets. Heavyset. Up to no bloody good, loafing close to the post office. He is about to step from the footpath and cross the road when he is approached by a man who has appeared suddenly from behind the car.

A young fella, younger than him. A pup. A *get*, as his batman would say. Another man emerges to join him, older, mature, hard-faced.

'Give us over the bag,' the younger man says. 'Throw it to the side.'

'Do it and you'll live,' his older colleague says, aiming a revolver.

He jumps at the younger man, hitting him square with his fist in the chin, and almost on top of the older one he sees the dark eye of the revolver …

At the inquest, the old officer listens to the details surrounding his only son's murder. A motor was hired for 15s from Kennedy's Garage down Bang-Up Lane in Kildare and a driver provided. His son was shot in the head in a struggle and robbed. The driver was forced at gunpoint to drive towards Tully, in the direction of Kildoon, where he dropped the men off. He returned to Kildare and met with Detective Inspector Queenan and spun his yarn. For yarn is what it is. Graham said he did not recognise the men. A lie. His boss, who rented the car, did not know the men either. A lie. Daly, a young mechanic, said two young men entered the garage to hire a car and gave descriptions of them. They know the names, all right, but they are afraid to say so – in the open, at any rate.

They had to let the men they arrested go for lack of evidence.

He sighs and listens a little more intently to the proceedings.

The coroner says, 'What occurred then – after the first man went to confront the officer?'

'The officer jumped to catch hold of the first man.'

'And you were told at this point to start the car?'

'Yes.'

'Who ordered you to start the car?'

'This other man got in beside me and ordered me to start the car. He had a revolver.'

'Was this before or after the shot was fired?'

'After.'

'These men – they never mentioned each other by name?'

'No.'

'What did the other men say when they got into the car?'

'One of them said, "Well, that fella is done anyhow."'

'What else?'

'They told me to drive out by the nunnery.'

'And they threatened you – tell me what they said, exactly.'

'They told me that if I went to identify them in any way that there was more than three of them in it, and they would get me sometime.'

He stays to hear it all, the aftermath, the autopsy report, every single detail. By the time he has heard all that there is to hear, in addition to being heartbroken, he is thoroughly heart-sickened.

Such a waste of life. He was only twenty-two and far too brave for his own good.

If there is consolation – and it is purely consolation – he finds it in the conversation he had with General Michael Collins in the aftermath of his son's funeral. 'Please, find the men who did this to John. Don't let them get away.'

And Michael Collins's response held the steel of a true promise. 'Francis, I give you my word. We'll root them out from under their stones – we'll deal severely with anyone who is even remotely connected to this.' One officer to another, the chief of staff of the nation's fledgling army to an elderly soldier of the old order. This is his consolation. His son's death will be avenged.

Chalky

15 December 1922

He awakens, listens to what he thinks in the drift towards full consciousness is the noise of a disturbed sea.

For a slide of milliseconds he is someplace else, and then he realises where he is and what had stolen him from sleep. The wind, dancing with trees and most likely turning in on itself too. *Like … yes, like … us. Christ. Another day. How much longer will I have to spend in this fucking silage pit?* He turns on his side in his bed and faces the wall. He touches the coarse brick with his fingertips, then spreads the palm of his hand against it, feels its coldness. Withdraws his hand. A habit from childhood, this reaching out in search of a boundary, to reassure himself that there is only one side of the bed from which he can accidentally fall. He had not slept for long. A couple of hours, not much more than that. He had lain awake after lights out, turning thoughts in his head, all the time returning to the one thought: *You're for it now, lad.* He had prayed to Jesus Christ Almighty and every saint his mother begs, cajoles and bullies for this to end in a way other than how he had been told it would end. Than how his inner voices often tell him.

I knew from the outset, he thinks. *And yet I chose not to know or believe.*

His mouth is dry, his lips rimmed with scum he rubs off with the side of his forefinger. He is cold under the thin layers of grey blankets, grey with black stripes across the top and bottom. Rank markings of sorts. Dirty and stained with old and hard snot and whitish and silverish streaks like a snail's trail. At least the sheets are clean. Stiff as the lid of a coffin.

The wind continues to imitate the sound of the restless sea. For a few moments it had been a pleasure for him to imagine that he was in Courtown, staying with his Aunt Eileen. Sea watching, sea listening, shell gathering. Skimming stones, licking ice cream, biting off the end of the cone and sucking through the funnel, crunching the wafer tight as a sat-upon sandwich, tongue visiting the corners of his lips.

They say it's definitely going to happen. They say they're to be made an example of. They say there's no turning back. And yet in spite of all they say, he does not believe them. He will not allow himself to lose that bit of hope.

An example? They mean as a warning to his side. A warning not to mess with them – we boys mean business. *So did we.*

He wonders what time it is. Darkness tells you little.

You won't miss your mother till she's gone. You won't miss your son till he's dead. You won't miss your time till there's none. Or stolen. Or you do something to surrender it.

Should have listened to my mother and walked away.

'You're eighteen, Chalky, what do you know of life? Do you think you know more than me? By Jasus, you've a long way to go, son, before you even begin to learn half of what I know.'

'Will you stop, Mam? Leave us alone.'

'Alone, is it? You didn't ask me to leave ye alone when Thos wanted to hide revolvers in my shed.'

'You'd try the patience of a saint.'

'You've done your bit – the odds are stacked against ye. I don't like what that shower have done, but by Christ—'

'Give over.'

'This shenanigans will be the rock you perish on – mark my words, son.'

Mark my words.

Just as daylight begins to filter through, a bird begins its song. He likes to think of it as a robin, but it's probably not. Things rarely, if ever, square up to your hopes and expectations. The arched window, its acute semi-circle of glass and sturdy iron bars, affords him a small view of the prison yard, a patch of December sky. Yesterday morning, his first in the Glasshouse, he had tried to catch sight of the bird, to see what else there was to see. Nothing to make a lad stir himself from bed, surrender the tiny heat in him.

They'll know for sure today. It'll be stamped, Mangan had said yesterday. Meaning their fates will be sealed. Mangan isn't the optimistic sort. He puts his money on horses and immediately regrets it, saying that the fucking thing hasn't got a prayer of winning. He's often more right than he is wrong. Could be he's wrong about this, too. But Mangan's not a worrier and when you see a non-worrier worrying, drawing into himself like a retreating shadow, then you've reason for concern.

His cell. This prison. They call it the Glasshouse because of its glass roof. It has a proper name but no one calls it that, so he figures its real title is of no bloody importance. There are sixty-four cells, two storeys, floorboards – twelve-foot-tall external walls and a main gate of double doors. Built by the British over sixty years ago. When they turned the key on him the first night, he stood in his cell near numb with shock. There he stood: sore in the ribs from a soldier's boot, cold-bellied from what he had witnessed happen to Thos. Thinking that he'd never been locked up anywhere and how the clanging door had not alone restricted his movement, but had also allotted him a portion of air to breathe. Air his lungs would breathe in and out, over and over. Four walls of cold brick. A smell of piss from the pot under the bed. Living with the smell of his own slop when the fear gripped hold of his bowel.

Down the road a short distance from the Glasshouse is Hare Park Internment Camp, where hundreds of others fighting the same cause as himself are interned – in the aftermath of their arrest, his column were detained in a wooden hut there while the redcaps cleared cells for them in the Glasshouse. IRA, Irregulars, anti-Treaty forces. Once part of the same soul, now torn away – the terrible twin. The internees catcalled the redcaps and soldiers and shouted *Good on ye* to them, but he didn't think they'd done anything special. Unless being stupid enough to get caught could be regarded as something special.

'Yese are fucked, boys,' a redcap said, not in a cruel manner, but matter of factly and quietly, which in itself was a form of cruelty.

The longest day will be today. And there might be longer ahead. Seemingly longer, at any rate. The Glasshouse is stirring to life, if life in prison can be rightly called a stirring to life. Routine – a stirring to routine. He is merely a couple of days here and yet he understands the concept and definition of monotony – what Thos had spoken of when he had been interned in the Rath camp in 1921. Boredom. Sheer bloody boredom. Even boredom ends. There is consolation in that, but not much, he thinks. Depends on how it ends, what brings it all to an end. In the yard, the din of feet snapping to attention and of orders being pitched in a loud voice, of a new guard being mounted for duty and the old guard standing down, kitchen noises and smells of steaming porridge, boiled eggs and wet tea leaves and a fry for the Governor replace the song of the small bird.

Here in individual cells are men caught with him in the trench, save for two, and no one knows where they got to or what has become of them: Pat Mangan, Bryan Moore, Pat Bagnall, Joey Johnston, Pat Nolan, James O'Connor. Johnston, like him, is eighteen, while

Bagnall is nineteen. Moore replaced Thos Behan as the column's officer. The others are older, ranging from mid-twenties to thirty-seven.

They slop out, empty their chamber pots – those that need to. Many veteran internees don't, as they had trained their systems into holding its waste till their cell doors breathe out, in a toilet on the ground floor, under the eye of the redcaps.

Each eats his meal in his cell, but Chalky has no appetite. His nails are bitten to the quick, sore and raw at the thumb. Both thumbs. *If I don't get out of here soon … What the fuck was I thinking of, getting involved in all of this? How's Mam keeping? Anto? Seanie? What led me here? You forget? Well, think on it, boy.* This inner voice belongs to Brother Pius, a Christian Brother in the De La Salle school in Kildare town. A hard, hardy man who hated the English and with a tongue of fire railed off the sins and crimes they'd perpetrated against the Gael down the centuries. He taught history and Latin and his grey eyes had a glint you wouldn't see in a lunatic on a good day for the lunatic. He bet the face off Mangan for having a smirk, not knowing Mangan long enough to know that he had been born with a smirk. Six of the best was a lie he told the pupils – for he never gave less than six across the palm and two across the back of the hand for good measure, which hurt worse than the palm and left some boys with skinned knuckles. You had to do little or nothing to earn punishment. Just filling a space in the classroom was reason enough. 'Stop snivelling, boy, I haven't touched a stick to you yet.' 'Quit it or I'll boil your ear with a good thump.' 'Bare up and take it like a man. You'd hardly cut the grade as one of Fionn's warriors, would you, lad?'

You forget!

He paces his cell. The steam leaves his porridge and milky tea. His egg runny, not hard-boiled like he prefers. And remembers …

He was born Stephen Martin White on 9 January 1904, the oldest of three boys. His earliest memories of life are of his mother cradling him on her knee by a blazing turf fire after his father had scolded him for something he can no longer recall. His father, Charlie, though some called him Sonny, was thin and bony and always coughed after he'd spoken. He smoked a pipe and liked to spit into the fire and watch the goblets sizzle on the face of turf or a log. His dark hair was shot through with grey and he'd a slightly crooked chin. He tossed coins in a laneway down by the hotel and sometimes he won but more often he lost. He drank porter the days of the week and whiskey at Christmas or whenever he had a cold, and after he turned forty he got a lot of colds. Sonny worked at the horses, mucking out, riding work for Henry Brazil who had a stable on the Rathbride road, out over the first railway bridge as you leave Kildare train station.

He wasn't a Kildare man by origin but hailed from Rush in County Dublin. He never mentioned his parents. He didn't like Henry Brazil and had a falling out with him over the grooming of a grey colt. Chalky thought there was more to this than met the eye and a year after his father died his mother told him that his father sometimes had too much to say for his own good, and for the good of his family.

'A man who hasn't got any money in his pockets can't afford to have an opinion that's going to vex his betters,' she said.

'It wasn't about the grooming of a horse so?' he said.

'No – the stable had a winner down the country and Henry and your father shared a few drinks in the local hostelry and you know what your father was like when he had drink taken. No better patriot was he than when he had liquor coursing through his veins – what he wouldn't do to the English if he had a gun in his hands and all that sort of thing. And saying this to an English squire too – the eejit.'

His father was a stubborn man with the straight vision of a blinkered horse. The last barks of his coughs – God, it was awful to hear – the rasping, grating, blowing, the wheezing … the sight and reek of green phlegm, smell of warm honey, of menthol, medicines that helped, but only a little. God, there is such relief in silence, the quiet murmurs of women at prayer, the preparation for burial. The sickly sweet smell of death.

His father died six months after leaving work. Chalky was six years old. His mother threw his father's clay pipe and his few ounces of tobacco into the fire, burned his clothes in the backyard and drank the last dregs from the jar of whiskey.

'No more of that,' she said, 'or I'll have a red nose like Father Swan.'

He grew up in a home that had never known its fill of anything good, bad or indifferent. A fact of constant solace to his mother, comparing her misfortunes to the ones that had befallen a few of their neighbours, relatives and friends. However, there was always a scraping to make up the price of a dinner. A neighbour, a man who had never married, was a frequent visitor to their small cottage, always bringing a few vegetables he had grown in his large back garden that touched an embankment that sloped toward railway tracks. As Chalky added on in years, Mr Wilson's visits became less frequent, as though it didn't seem right that the man for whom his mother now worked part time – cleaning his house, washing his clothes – should be so often on his employee's property.

Wilson had the thickest black hair he'd ever seen, a round-eyed man who had large stick-out ears. He treated Chalky and his brothers as though they were his friends. There was nothing authoritarian about him and he never once interrupted Breege whenever she reproached her sons, though in the soft light of the evening fire he would tell her to go aisy on the lads. Regarding history and the War of Independence and the Civil War, he said it was wise to keep out of it. For the poor man never wins and 'tis him and some of the rich who think war a game who did all the fighting and bleeding. He liked to mete out advice such as, 'Never trust a man who peppers his conversation with "I'll be honest with you" or "I'll give it to you straight".'

Chalky spent a lot of his childhood in the park, playing football for the local team. He never took a liking to hurling, went off the game entirely when he lost half of a front tooth to a fellow who was renowned for having a wild and careless swing. No, the football was better. Better a fist in your gob than a stick. He played midfield, though he was slight and not as tall as others he competed against. But he was quicker than most over five yards and rarely landed himself in trouble, evading tackles that would have broken a less speedy player.

Would he and Mangan be out in time to start winter training with the club?

His mother came from Ferns and had a younger sister called Eileen who married well. Her husband owned a hotel in Courtown. Every summer into their early teens, Mam and Eileen picked strawberries and raspberries and made jam which they sold on the roadside along with punnets of fruit they'd secreted from the fruit farm in a hessian sack. They lived in a house that looked across a narrow road and past the ruins of an abbey to the River Slaney, where his Uncle Michael's body was found entangled in rushes where the Black and Tans had thrown him. They shot him for breaking curfew, the bullet hitting his heart. No questions asked. No warning. The fish had gone with his eyes. Mam said she'd never forget that image – an awful one to own of her brother.

Chalky was fourteen when the war in Europe

came to an end. He knew to see a couple of the men from town who had gone to fight and die in the trenches. Mam and a few of the neighbours said they were traitors for fighting England's war, for fighting with the murderers of Pearse and Connolly. Every man jack of them ought to be taken out across the plains and shot and buried under furze bushes with nare a marker to indicate the whereabouts of their traitorous bones.

Sheila, their neighbour, said, 'I'd sooner eat stones in my backyard than eat food bought with the King's shilling.'

'I spoke to Maura when I heard Liam had joined,' Mam said, 'but she put me out of the house, said her son was doing a fine thing by putting bread on the family table.'

'Who'll do it for her now?' Sheila said.

Mam said, 'Well, I hope God never sends that cross to my door – to lose her son.'

'I've no doubt, Breege, none of ours would ever rally to the Union Jack.'

There was no sigh of regret when telegrams arrived at the soldiers' homes or the usual cry of 'God pity him and them' and suchlike, as it was more or less regarded that they'd reaped what they'd sown. Silence said so. And absence from the homes of the bereaved.

He began to mitch from school when he was thirteen to avoid the attention of the Christian Brothers. One might as well be beaten for skipping school as for simply being present. If the day was fine and sunny, they'd hide out in a clearing in furze in the Curragh plains, an undulating grasslands of almost 5,000 acres. They'd eat jam sandwiches, share brown bottles of stout and Woodbines and talk the hours away. He remembers Mangan sitting in the furze with his legs stretched out and ankles crossed, socks folded over the rims of his leather ankle boots, hand propped behind him like a tent peg, the other holding his cigarette, the eye of which he studied now and then, like it held answers or advice. Squinting as he spoke about getting a job with the railway and that he wouldn't be going to school for much longer, how he pitied Chalky for having another couple of years to put up with in that bloody place. Johnston and Bagnall were there, too, but there were others also from time to time, faces now with no names attached. Passing round of the brown bottle, sandwiches, fag ends, a ritual of sorts and therefore the creation of a bond that carried over onto the football field and determined on which side he fought for in the Civil War. It was Mangan who, four years later in the Harp pub, talked him into joining the local column.

'I don't know, Pat. Collins, you know, he's no fool.'

'Why should we quit when we're so close to getting the whole island free? We can't leave the north to those bastards.'

'But this is something to build on, Pat. Twenty-six counties now, the rest later. Like Collins said.'

'Bollocks to that – you can't seriously believe that shite.'

Chalky didn't know his own mind on the matter – he was for one side one moment and the other the next. He wanted to be with his friends and he liked the excitement and the togetherness of the whole thing, feeling wanted and a part of something – his decision more an indecision and yet this too was a decision; to see how things go.

So he trained with the fragments of a column that had fought in the War of Independence, in the hilltop woods overlooking the town, was given a hurling stick to use as a rifle and taught the principles of shooting by Thos. They raided shops in the town over and over and bought Lee Enfields from a Free State soldier in Naas Barracks. Often his mother reproached him, saying he was to walk away from that nonsense. Once she went to a pub and chastised him in front of Thos and Moore, but Thos smiled and said he'd mind him like a son and she had to settle for this because Chalky had two pints in front of him and was brazening her out the door with his father's hard look.

During the day, four of the column worked in the railway station in Kildare and so knew all of what moved on the lines. At night they fought against the forces of the newly formed provisional government that paid them their weekly wage.

Chalky thought of this irony, how perhaps it was tinted with some hypocrisy, but he kept this to himself. He supposed Wilson was right when he said there was no such thing as a clean war – all wars are dirty. Still, it was not how he would prefer things; to take money with one hand and shoot the giver with the other.

Locomotives were derailed and goods carriages robbed. Free State soldiers sniped at as they travelled down the lines to the south, bringing reinforcements and supplies.

Wogan Browne – his killing – well, his mother went off the wall entirely and said if he'd had anything to do with it, he was not to show his face to her again.

'I hadn't, Ma. I swear to God.'

'Who killed him? Who was it?'

'I don't know – I wasn't there.'

'It wasn't you?'

'No, I said. Didn't I just swear to you?'

He had never been told who killed the officer, though he had his suspicions. He'd been busy digging that day, since morning – digging that stupid hole. A young man pulled the trigger is all he knew for definite. That could apply to six in his column and some other fellas around the town, fly-by-nights who drifted in whenever it suited them, who Thos had run a few of the nights because he hadn't seen them for an age. These fellas were it in for themselves – who didn't mind the robbing of shops but didn't want anything to do with serious fighting.

By all accounts, the officer would be alive today if he hadn't acted the hero.

They wounded some soldiers on the night trains. When Chalky heard of this the following day, he wondered if it had been his bullets that had found the mark. It was hard to tell as it was pitch black and conditions had been very wet and windy. After the attack they went to the widow's farmhouse.

Thos knew a woman who lived in a farmhouse close to Moore's Bridge about a mile and a half down the line from town. Chalky, Mangan and O'Connor lifted the floorboards and spent days digging out a trench in which they hid themselves when necessary and unnecessary and also their supplies and equipment.

'I don't like this at all,' Mangan said, 'hiding in a long hole like this. What hope would you have of escaping if you'd a need to?'

As it turned out, none.

As the morning grows strong in itself, as the sky loses its scraps of blue and turns grey and the metallic smell of rain permeates the walls, she comes to him in his mind's eye. His heart's scrap of blue.

She is about thirty-five but looks older, marks of a hard life in the lines that ring her eyes, almost touching her high cheekbones. She comes from a large family that farms a few scrubby acres down the bog road leading from the Japanese Gardens. A respectable family.

She smiles a lot and is always upbeat, the true sign of someone putting on a brave act. She has green eyes, a pretty oval face, the pride of herself, her hair that she keeps long and pony-tailed. She has a substance to her that you will not find in many others. She is bubbly, outgoing, brazen tongue laden with innuendo. Insightful too. He'd caught her a couple of times looking past things at things.

'You're too young for me, boy,' she said as he caught up with her on the town's main street on a busy Thursday market day, smiling. 'Far too young.'

'I am not.'

'Are you not?'

'No.'

'What would you do with a woman like me?' She looked sidelong at him. Her eyebrow on the rise. He felt his cheeks burn. 'When you make up your mind, let me know,' she said, turning the corner at the chemist shop.

Days later, he let her know. He said he'd treat her like a lady, which elicited a wry smile from her.

'A lady,' she said. 'That'll be interesting. And how do you treat your ladies?'

'I respect her, buy her flowers, perfume, chocolates,' he said, clueless, because he hadn't an idea of what he should say. He'd thought it enough to tell her, enough for her to know that he was serious about her. He blushed when he reran her question in his mind. *How do you treat your ladies?*

He'd never kissed a woman on the lips.

'I see,' she said. 'But not too respectful, Chalky – I wouldn't like that at all.' The evening he was to meet her, he was captured. Eight o'clock, they'd arranged to meet in her sister's house that was empty for the night.

When my luck is flat, it's truly flat.

His eyes are fixed on Alice as the redcap enters his cell.

'Up off your arse, and don't look at me like that or you'll be spitting splinters out of your hole.' The redcap taps his baton against the wall. 'I said, get up off your lazy arse.'

He eases his feet to the floor and into his black shoes, still caked with mud where he'd slipped in the tracks made by the soldiers' lorry at Moore's Bridge.

'Where am I going?'

'To the exercise yard – ye need to get some air into ye. A waste of good fucking air, if you ask me.'

Her name is Alice Donovan and when he first held her hand he noticed how the veins on its back formed a prominent H.

'Move, for Christ's sake. I've seen two-legged sheep move quicker.'

Alice …

They come together in the yard, the seven. Raindrops begin to fall like the last drops being squeezed from a wet rag. There are other prisoners who linger with the group until they sense that their presence is unwanted. Embarrassed and apologetic, they hurry along. A red-haired lad not wise to the atmosphere is asked by Moore to give the group a few minutes together.

Moore leans his back to the wall, puts the heel of his foot to it, draws on his cigarette. He calls for the others to hush and again when their whispers weren't hush enough. One of his eye teeth is yellowy, the bottom row a line of crooked headstones above a rim of thin lip.

'Listen in,' he says. His voice strong but with a quaver, like a current appearing in waters Chalky had always known to be calm. Against the chatter of the other prisoners circling around them, the pitter-patter of rain on corrugated iron, they strain their ears so as not to drop a single word.

'We're in bad shape with this, boys. I was talking to a redcap and he says we're for the bullet. We all saw what Kearney did to Thos, okay?' He let those words linger for a few seconds and then continues. 'We all knew the score regarding the weapons amnesty, lads, so there isn't much point in crying about it. I expect every one here, if worse comes to worse, to behave like a soldier, to honour the cause we fought for and not to go down like a coward. That's an order.'

He glances at each pair of eyes in turn and adds, 'Is that understood?'

In return, they either nod under his gaze or mumble, 'Yes.'

'Any questions?' he says.

Mangan raises his hand.

'Fire away, Pat.'

'Do you think we're done for because we seen what Kearney did to Thos?'

Moore's mouth opens, then closes. He had already said as much without actually saying it. We all know, Chalky thinks. Why the fuck does everything have to be written out for Mangan? He pucks Mangan lightly in the ribs; Mangan ignores the touch.

'It doesn't help us that we're witnesses to a murder,' Moore says.

'But there were soldiers around too.'

'A couple of officers and a sergeant, Pat. The rest weren't there to see anything. They were busy dealing with Nora and her daughters.'

'But—'

Moore cuts in. 'Look. Art Kearney is dangerous and worse than dangerous since our boys killed his brother in the Baltinglass ambush, right? Buckley is the other officer I know of – he killed four or five of ours in Kerry – and the other officer, I don't know who he is, or the sergeant. They'll not leap to our defence, you can be sure of that.'

'Jesus!' O'Connor says, as if he has just woken up to the seriousness of their predicament.

'What?' Moore asks.

'A fucking raindrop is after going down my spine.'

A ripple of uneasy laughter. In the grey light, at Moore's sudden turn and then fix of his head, Chalky sees the yellowy bruise under the commandant's eye. Notices too how he keeps staring at his feet as if he were imagining what it will be like for them to never again feel newly cut grass.

It is Johnston who asks what each intended to ask. 'Where's Hennigan and Dooley?'

They had been in the cottage with them.

'I have no idea.'

'Did they fucking hang us out to dry?' O'Connor asks.

'The searchlight …' Nolan says, hoping that it was the great arm of light from the water tower that reached across the Curragh landscape for miles and not the tongues of their comrades that had done for them.

'I don't know where they are or why they're not

with us,' Moore says.

Chalky says, 'Eddie wasn't in the trench. Dooley was.'

This is true, he thinks, thinking back – Dooley was ushered up and out of the trench and followed Hennigan through the kitchen door, guided by soldiers who slapped their rifle butts against their arms and cursed them in and out of the ground. Then Thos said something under his breath to Kearney and the officer walked to the edge of the trench and loosened a round from his Webley revolver into Thos. The peace of silence, the stink of cordite, the splatter of blood, the glassy, shocked look in Thos's eyes, clutching his arm. Death came for Thos a few minutes later when he found his voice and refused to climb onto the bed of the lorry.

'Dispatch that bollocks,' Art Kearney said to another officer. Pushed and kicked yards from the lorry, into Curragh darkness, a single shot rang out. Silence and then uproar. And the soldiers in the truck beat the protests out of us with rifle butt and muzzle, Chalky thinks, his ribs rightly fucking rattled.

Mangan says, 'I think one or the other or both of them ratted on us. Dooley likes to talk – he could have said something that was picked up by the wrong person. As for Hennigan, I don't know him. Would he talk? Did he point the finger at us, or was it Nora?'

'Does it matter? Does it matter at all now?' Bagnall says dejectedly. 'Knowing anything like that isn't going to save us.'

Mangan goes to speak, but a redcap's whistle blow silences him. Breaking away, they join the shuffling mass towards the grey double doors.

'Remember, heads up, okay?' Moore says, his own not so high.

Back in his cell, Chalky dries his rain-wet hair and drinks tea. He holds rosary beads that a redcap had given him, a Cork man who said he hated this place and the war and that he had a son the same age as Chalky back in Cobh. Some of the redcaps were good fellas and others were cold and austere and hard-faced. They'd no give in their hearts. Like Moore and a few of the lads with whom he served – little or no give, cliff faces the sea wouldn't soften and crumble in a thousand years.

He stares at the locked door and wonders if the kindly redcap had already heard of the decision. The rain gives way to hail.

He remembers the night before they were captured. The rain teemed and was taken by the wind into places that old people said had never got wet before, except for a drunk who might have pissed there. The wind swirled so you couldn't put a direction to it. Before Nora's farmhouse, the column operated out of a shed a short distance into a lane, flanked on one side by stone stables with green doors, an old place that hadn't seen a horse for years, a loft starved of hay – home to cobwebs and odds and ends of cart parts.

He had asked Alice to meet him there that evening. She did but said that she couldn't stay for long as she'd to accompany her mother to a neighbour's wake. At her age she wasn't great on her feet and needed the lend of a steady arm and another pair of feet to help her get about. 'You look like you have no bother getting about,' he said, putting his hands on her hips.

He was much taller than her, and he was by no means tall.

'Don't be cheeky. I'm only twenty-eight.'

He didn't know much about women, but he knew enough not to ever dispute something like her age. 'You don't look it,' he lied.

'I'm in my mid-thirties,' she said quietly, like a ghost to itself. He remained silent and then she moved on to something else. She wore a green coat and a navy and white scarf round her neck. A cold sore in the corner of her lip held pink ointment. She had skinny legs and he thought of them parted and felt a surge of excitement, himself stiffen. He went to her.

'No,' she said. 'Tomorrow. I promise.'

'Here?'

'No – my sister has gone to the seaside. Her house will be empty tomorrow.'

'Good.'

She wouldn't kiss him but pointed to her cheek for him to kiss there. They embraced and he cupped her breast and for sweet moments she clung to him hard and he thought her promise might be fulfilled there and then.

'No,' she gasped, 'not here, not …' Her cheeks had flushed. Her coat smelled of rain.

'What time?' he asked, the hunger for her wild in him.

'Around eight, okay?'

He frowned.

'Is there a problem?'

'I might be a little late.'

'Why?'

'I'm helping a man to paint a house.'

'Running with the boys, are we?'

'I'm painting a house.'

She reached forward and put the tip of her forefinger to his upper lip. 'I like a man who can keep things to himself.' She meant about them, for she'd be disgraced for taking up with a lad half her age. If their ages were reversed, nothing would have been thought of it. She gave him her sister's address and the direction, though there was no need for he knew who lived in all the houses in town and those on the outskirts. He was to knock three times on the front window.

'Bring a couple of bottles, will you?' she said.

'Nothing surer.'

When she was gone, he hurried a cigarette to his lips and went outside to smoke. He spent some time looking at the stars, the cut of the moon, at the dark clouds following each other. *Jesus*, he thought, *don't let me piss meself, don't let me let myself down* … Strange, he thought, to be praying to Jesus for a sin to successfully happen.

At home that evening, Mam and his brothers had remarked upon the weight he had lost. They were right. His trousers had loosened at the waist and were baggy around the backside.

'It's easy to see why,' Mam said, spooning tealeaves into a teapot. It was. He lived on tea and cigarettes. Touched nothing only his fingernails whenever the column was an hour or so away from launching an attack. Thos didn't call them attacks – they were reprisals. A typed communiqué from Command would arrive and he'd read it aloud and then pass it around the column as though to prove he was not inventing these orders: disrupt railway lines, attack Free State troops whenever and wherever you can with whatever force you can muster. Watch out for the plainclothes.

Some nights he wet the bed, even when he'd had nothing to drink from five in the evening. It happened whenever he was more anxious and nervous than usual, after he'd held his Lee Enfield rifle, fed its two magazine clips of five rounds into the breech and used the bolt action and fired at a target. There was a thrill in this, a fear, a godly feeling, a feeling of power, and also a terrible coldness that gripped his belly and advanced a need for him to tell the lads he had to shit in the furze, while the truth was he had to throw up. But he would have died sooner than talk of these things, for he was one of the lads and none of them would want to lose face in front of the others. That was unthinkable!

He had seen a dead man with bullet holes in him. The flesh torn from him in chunks, his face blown away allowing you see the gristle under his nose, the teeth smashed and parted from the gums. No one knew his name or where he had come from, only that he had done this to himself. One of theirs. Curiously, he did not feel ill in his stomach at the sight. He went through a sort of macabre wondering and some slight concern at how easy it was to end your life. Easy in the sense that it didn't require much effort to chamber bullets and squeeze a trigger – it was the lead-up to it, the torment, that must have been impossibly difficult. Crossing the Rubicon, as the Christian bastard Brother used say; the point of no return.

His mother, who washed his sheets, said he probably felt the cold more than most, that his grandfather, her father, had been plagued by a pair of bad kidneys all his born days. That whatever killed you in this life had probably killed others in your family line.

'I know you,' Alice had said in the park the next morning as they walked past embankments grown woolly with grass. This was an accidental on purpose meeting, both setting off for walks on a route each knew the other travelled.

'How know me?'

She said he was shy, acted tough but was far from it. He bothered himself with minor detail so as to avoid bothering with major issues. Unsure of himself, uncertain, always asking questions about small matters, interrupting his superiors as they discussed problems.

'Enough for you?' she said.

'Enough,' he said quietly, abruptly veering toward the gate. She called his name, caught up with him, jerked at his elbow for him to stop.

'Don't you ever walk away from me,' she said.

She knows me and yet wants to be with me in spite of knowing me, he'd thought. He'd felt good about that and a little apprehensive, too.

'I want you to come earlier tomorrow – earlier than eight o'clock. Forget about the bloody painting.'

'I can't.'

'Yes, you can. Come down about four – I'll have a lovely tea and—'

He shook his head.

'Four o'clock or don't come at all.'

'Ah, will you leave it for eight, and if I can get there earlier I will. Promise.'

She wasn't happy with this compromise but she softened and said, 'Don't come near me if you're loaded with drink – I hate the smell of the stuff off a man.'

'I'm painting. Not drinking.'

In her was the angry red of the skies – no doubting it – when his three knocks on the window didn't happen. In fact, he was angry, too, but his anger was tinged with a terrible sense of loss and disappointment.

In the hall mirror, in paltry light cast by the oil lamp, he looked like someone he had never seen before. A stranger to himself, someone who could not bring himself to look him in the eye. He had on his flat cap, a grey trench coat and black shoes Mam had bought for him from Flea Daly at the market. He fixed the belt on his coat, tightening it a notch, and called back into the house, 'See yese later – don't go waiting up.' He did not like his mother to see him off, did not like to see the pleading in her eyes for him to stay put, to stay with his brothers, stay warm in the house and not to be going playing havoc with his life and that of others. 'Don't be making a bandit of yourself,' she liked to say whenever she wanted to madden him in turn for his maddening her.

'Where are you going, Chalky?' Mam said, following him to the front gate. As if she did not know. It was a little after five in the evening and already dark. There was a strong smell of turf smoke. No breeze. A crop of stars, a cat meowing, a dog's distant bark. And yet the night felt *empty*. His sigh hawed the air.

'I have a right to know, Chalky,' she said, gathering

her black shawl around her shoulders, the collar of it torn but it was her favourite, given her many Christmases ago by Eileen. He had her blue eyes, though in hers there was a softness and a sadness at her failure to keep close to her a son who for his own sake needed to be kept close.

'I'm out, painting a—'

'Don't spin me that rigmarole.'

'Thos was asking for you.'

'I don't care about that man, nice as he is. I want you to stay here with me this evening. I have a mother's bad feeling in my bones.'

'Sure, you get a bad feeling in your bones about everything.'

'I do not.'

He stamped his feet and rubbed his hands. 'I better be going.'

'Will I keep you dinner?'

He shook his head. 'I won't be home this evening. I've to go somewhere else after.'

'I see,' she said.

'So don't be worrying.'

'With your woman, is it – the town bicycle?'

She may as well have run his heart through with a red-hot poker.

'Shut your mouth about Alice, Mam.'

'You're determined to make a complete and utter bags of your life.'

'She's okay. I like her.'

'She's too well liked.'

'Ah sure, the way the world is, some of us have to be bad.'

'At the end of the day it's all down to that – what you think and no one else.'

'I haven't got the time for this. I need to be on my way.'

'Ask yourself why she hasn't settled with a man.'

'She's only just met the right one.'

Before she could respond, he reached out a hand and rested it on her shoulder and squeezed. 'Mam, leave it lie – just leave it.'

She felt a cord tighten in her throat and tears gather. Though it was in her to say a lot more, she understood he would not listen and she did not want to see him leave in a huff. For the last memory of them being together to be one fraught with tension and harsh words. Every time he left the fireside to run with the column, there was a chance that he might not return. She nodded. 'You'll miss your train,' she said with an edge she hadn't intended.

Mangan and Johnston were waiting for him in Jackie's Lane, down from the red-brick Railway Hotel. His bones drank in the cold. He wished he'd eaten the potato soup and brown bread his mother had put before him. It might have fortified his blood against the pervading chill.

'What the fuck kept you?' Mangan said, coming from the depth of darkness into the half-light cast by the hotel's yard light.

'I had to take a piss.'

'Jesus, you're full of the stuff,' Johnston said, emerging at Mangan's shoulder.

'We'll make tracks so,' Mangan said.

'Do you know something, lads? I'm really not feeling the best,' Chalky said.

'You're a bit pale looking all right,' Mangan said as they left the lane and began to cross the road.

'Yellow, you mean,' Johnston said.

'Watch your mouth or you'll be having it sown up,' Chalky said.

'Try it and I'll put you in a fucking shroud, ya fucking mammy's boy.'

'Shut it! Any fucking more of this and I'll do the two of ye,' Mangan said.

A resentful silence ensued for a few seconds.

'Look – I've a date, right.'

'With who?' Mangan asked.

'Yer one,' Johnston said. 'Alice Donovan. Sure, hadn't he got her out in the stables yesterday evening.'

For fuck sake, Chalky thought, a lad can't piss crooked around here but everyone gets to know of it.

'Her?' Mangan said.

'Alice,' Chalky said.

Mangan pulled up abruptly in front of the other two and planked his large, hand flat on Chalky's chest. 'Chalky boy, sick or not, you're better off coming with us than going to see her. She wouldn't be good for you.'

Jesus, Chalky saw it – the jealousy in his friend's eyes, the pain... Still, he felt a pain too. Within the space of ten minutes three people had belittled someone for whom he had feelings. Funny how he hadn't heard anything of Alice's reputation until he had started seeing her. Yet what if it were true of her, what they were saying? Why say such things if they weren't? These questions bothered him because there was no way of knowing for sure if they were lies. Time will tell, he thought.

'I think I'll have to find that out for myself, boys,' he said, putting his hand on Mangan's wrist and bringing it down and away.

'Suit yourself. You've been advised,' Mangan said.

They vaulted a low stone wall into a field dense with thistles and nettles and cow shit and traversed north-east till they came to the railway tracks. They crossed them amidst the strong smell of creosote on the sleepers, the rough stones prodding at the soles of their feet, and turned east, towards the grasslands.

They walked quickly along a beaten grass trail called 'The Race of the Black Pig' since ancient times, through vast aprons of furze bush, muddy and slippery in places, left so by racehorses wending their way to the gallops from nearby stables. Chalky led the trio. He was lightest on his feet and knew the route – once Mangan had led them down a dead end in a blanket of furze and Johnston had brought them to a lone hawthorn tree where dogs had minutes beforehand reefed the stomach from a sheep and feasted on the aborted lamb. The night air was perfectly clear. On the far side of the tracks, the searchlight from the Curragh

Camp's dominant feature, the Water Tower, swept tremendous bars of light across the grassland. Last May he had gone to the Curragh to witness the handover of the camp by the British forces to the newly formed Irish Free State army. It pissed rain. Side by side walked the Irish and British staff officers along the camp's northernmost road to the Water Tower. Sir Dalrymple with his walking stick, his eyes fixed on the ground ahead of him, seemed in an awful hurry to have an unsavoury business done with. The tricolour was to be raised at noon, but when the British had lowered the Union Jack for the last time, they'd cut the mast and another had to be found. Wet and windy and though it was worth the drenching to see the tricolour flag stretch itself in the westerly blow, it had appalled him to hear whispers among the crowd regretting that the British had left the camp: 'We'll miss their money.' He'd had to resist the urge to give the man with two chins a hard dig to the nose.

Johnston snuffled and said he thought he heard the noise of a heavy engine, so they pulled up and listened. But all they heard was the heave of their own chests, the bleat of a sheep and the soft breeze strumming the wires on the telegraph poles.

'I hear nothing,' Mangan said.

'It sounded like the engine of a lorry,' Johnston said.

'There'd be no lorries on the road at night, not with the curfew,' Mangan said.

'Unless it belongs to the Free Staters,' Chalky said.

Again, they listened for several seconds.

'Lead on, Chalky,' Mangan said.

'Okay,' Chalky said.

'Okay,' Johnston laughed lowly.

'Okay,' Mangan said. 'Move it, ye fuckers.'

Okay. There was a joke behind the word, though it doesn't seem so funny now. But then, nothing does. As Mam likes to say, 'I'll put the smile the other side of your face.'

Fate had done it to the lot of them. Despite the fact that there was no requirement to, they crouched low. The light fell short of the railway tracks, which ran on a man-made embankment for a mile across the plains, tapering to ground level shortly before Moore's Bridge. The next station beyond this, less than a mile off, was the Curragh siding, used to deposit racegoers intended for the Curragh Racecourse and troops bound for the Curragh Camp. After this lay Newbridge Station and beyond this other little worlds that dotted the twenty-six miles or so to Dublin's Kingsbridge Station. They had fired upon the Curragh siding last week, injuring soldiers.

Coming to a road west of the bridge, Chalky walked on his hunkers to the edge of a furze bush and looked left and right. Listened. Jesus, all this listening, trying to detect human noise among the nocturnal ones issued by wildlife.

'All clear,' he breathed. 'Let's go.'

They darted across the road. They'd been on a quick walk for about forty minutes. Nora's farmhouse was down a boreen lined with tall hedging. Her brother, Paddy, was in Mountjoy and her father, Paddy Senior, had been vehemently opposed to the Treaty and had hanged himself from a rafter in the shed because he said he saw all too clearly the mayhem that was to lead on from the deal and wanted no hand, part or act in it. According to Thos, the old fella had been threatening to do away with himself for years and had finally found the balls to do so when told by his doctor that he was dying and hadn't long to live and to expect a deal of pain.

Mangan knocked on the oak door. Four loud knocks: Father, Son, Holy Ghost and the Pope – Nora's idea.

A few moments passed.

'Who is it?' Nora's voice, strong above her terrier's incessant barking.

'Mangan, and two.'

Bolts top and bottom were drawn and a key turned.

Nora was heavyset with netted grey hair. She wore a blue and white sleeveless kitchen coat spattered with white flour. She moved along the hall ahead of them, veins in her calves prominent through her tan tights.

Turning half about she said, 'Step in, boys. Patsy, give over that fecking barking, you're hurting the nerves in my head. Chalky put her out, will you, for a few minutes till I get to hear myself think.' Chalky picked up the small dog and went outside and let her down and watched as she lost herself in a thick privet hedge. Smiled. Then he sensed something – something not quite right – and a thought that seemed to have its source in the pit of his stomach roared at him to run, run, *run*.

He shook his head, rubbed his lips, heard the fall of feet coming towards him and froze, knees quivering as though the breeze of fear was withering them.

'O'Connor!' he said, relieved, when he recognised the Tipperary man's silhouette. The others accompanying him were Nolan, Bagnall and Dooley.

'Dooley the bollocks delayed us,' O'Connor said. 'A windy little fuck, that lad. Got his ma to tell us he was gone to Monasterevin, but I found him sitting up on a stool in the Harp – thought he was there guzzling porter for the night.'

Dooley walked past, pale-faced, eyes intent on avoiding others. Had he heard the voice too – *run, run, run?* Chalky walked in after them, shut and bolted the doors against the Curragh night. They were all in the long, wide kitchen, sitting around a rectangular pine table. The air was smoky from cigarette smoke and two bottles of Jameson sat on the table alongside a jug of water. Cheese, egg and corned beef sandwiches on blue-rimmed plates, a tin mug, sugar, milk and a caddied pot of tea for the sole non-drinker in the column: Hennigan. Chalky had always thought it odd that a sepia photograph of Queen Victoria should be hanging on a wall in the kitchen, though he supposed it was no less odd than a picture of the Sacred Heart in a home that truth told was not the least Christian.

Nora poured Jameson into whiskey glasses and passed them round to idle hands. Chalky sipped and felt the liquid warm the cold and unravel the knot in his stomach. Johnston was talking to Mangan about an article he had read in the newspaper concerning archaeologists discovering the tomb of an Egyptian pharaoh near Luxor.

'They went down these sixteen steps and opened the door and found all these golden statues and jewellery. I can't pronounce the pharaoh's name – it goes something like Tutankamun.'

'I heard about that,' Mangan said. 'The da was reading bits out to the ma.'

Moore rapped his fingers on the edge of the table and said, waving a plume of grey-blue smoke from his face, 'We're all here, Thos?'

'All accounted for.'

Chalky took in Thos's tobacco-stained fingers, how like his father's they were. Hennigan lifted the lid of the pot and whisked the leaves with a spoon. Vapour rose like a steal of fog across a bog. Poured. His forehead was afire with a rash of pimples.

'Right, lads – it's less than two weeks to Christmas, okay.'

Moore's habit of saying *okay*. It was something the younger lads in the column joked about when on their own.

'*Mangan, will you do that, okay?*'
'*Okay?*'
'*And Dooley, okay, let's get this done, okay?*'

Whenever anyone asked them what they thought of Moore they said, 'He's okay.'

'Now, okay,' he said, 'the Free Staters are starting to close in on us a little, okay. So we have to be extra careful and be a bit more selective about our choice of target – there's no doubt but we're hurting them – derailing the trains at Cherryville and the attack on the sidings have hampered their operations. We'll hit them once more before Christmas, okay. We're going to lash a convoy out of it as it moves towards Dublin, and—'

There was a noise. Moore looked at Nora and nodded for her to check its source.

'It's probably Patsy,' Chalky said. The dog had a habit of banging at the door whenever she wanted in.

Thos's face grew serious, 'In case it's not, move the table, boys, and get ready – come on out of that.'

Nora put her head round the door. 'I saw movement outside the sitting room window – too many shadows.'

Chalky felt his heart pitch sideways.

'Move it,' Thos whispered.

The table was lifted a few feet toward a maple kitchen unit and the floorboards lifted.

'Hennigan, you stay out and help Nora lift the table back into position – you're helping her on the farm. You know the spiel, boy,' Thos said. 'Spin it fucking well.'

Hurriedly, they filed into the trench, dropping to their hunkers. Chalky closed his eyes, his mind reciting a rosary of laments for not having heeded his inner voice. Run, even now, out the back door – a dozen strides and he'd be into the furze, wriggling through its woody underbelly of spine and skeleton, along the wood rot and sheep and fox shite. What a mess, eh? A stink, but fuck it, he would be free and not …

Floorboards dropped into place, the table dragged and lifted back into position, chairs properly arranged.

'Not a word,' Moore whispered, 'okay?'

Someone giggled. Another.

'Shush,' Thos said.

A fart. Some dirty nervous bastard farted and stank up the trench. The soldiers entered in a frenzied rush of stamping feet and raised voices, going from room to room, wardrobe doors opened and banged shut, beds turned on their sides. Nora's daughters shrieked – she never let them into the kitchen when the lads were there. One was slightly retarded and the other heavily pregnant for a married man in town.

'You!' a harsh voice said in the kitchen. 'Spread your hands against the wall.'

A second later: 'What's your name, boy?'

'Hennigan.'

'Where are you from?'

'Kildare town.'

Shuffling of feet, then moments later, 'He's nothing on him, sir.'

'Bring him outside and bring that fat bitch in here.'

But before this could happen another voice entered the kitchen. 'It's all right, Art, she's here. I did the searching on her – here. She was carrying all right.'

'Take your hands off me,' Nora's voice, hard and clear.

The noise of a slap across the face. Chalky recognised this from his schooldays and the Christian Brothers – Quick Draws, the class called them, like the cowboys they saw at the pictures.

'I give the orders here, not you. Carrying a Webley – sure, what the fuck would you be doing carrying that, missus?' His voice pitched higher. 'I want every inch of this house and the sheds searched – attics, haylofts, the lot!'

A soldier said, 'Yes, sir.'

Turning his attention to either Hennigan or Nora, the officer said, 'So, where are they?'

'Where's what?' Hennigan said.

'Soldier, are you going to let him speak to an officer like that?'

Crunch, snap of bone; a roar, pitiful. 'Oh Jesus, oh Jesus …'

'Missus, tell us or I'll put a bullet in his fucking head right now.'

Silence. Immediately, Chalky knew they were rumbled. So did the others, as there was a collective intake of warm, dusty trench air. Without a word spoken, they heard the table being drawn back.

'If youse don't come out, I'll shoot the boy first and then the woman.'

'Fuck it,' Moore said. 'The game's up, boys.'

'Jesus Christ,' said Thos.

The leaders, the column's commandants, raised the

floorboards and put them aside. While this was happening, the room filled with soldiers, all pointing their rifles into the trench.

'Out,' Kearney said. 'One at a time. You first. You next.'

'Kearney, you fucking bastard,' Thos said after glancing at Hennigan and his crushed face,

The officer calmly shot him. 'Shut your mouth,' he said.

Chalky's heart froze solid. 'Thos,' he said.

'You, get out!'

Chalky did as he was told and put his hands above and behind his head, but still the soldiers dug the heels of their rifles into his ribs and one kicked him there as they ran the gauntlet to the lorry.

'Buckley, Doorley, drag that cunt out of the dugout,' Kearney said in a loud voice.

Thos moaned, groaned and wheezed like something in him was going flat. It was as though parts of him were taking turns to announce their hurts. They carried him outside like farmers would haul a dead sheep between them, roughly, without thought.

At the tailboard, he saw Kearney, his wee sneer, and stole a giblet of blood and spit from his throat into his mouth and hawked it into Kearney's face. The officer did not flinch.

Silence then – in the lorry, amongst the soldiers, in every living creature – or at least so it appeared. A silence that made one think that every secret ever hidden under the stars was about to be revealed.

Then the soldiers birthed noise, shouting and cursing and slapping Thos across the back of his head. He was hauled away to the side of the lorry, into the darkness.

Pleas and shouts of *Don't you fucking dare, you bastards* … the report of the bullet silenced all talk, all moaning, all the loud nursing of hurts and grievances. And not just those of the prisoners.

A different silence to the other ensued.

Smashed …

'Ye fuckers!' Mangan roared, up on his feet but quickly beaten down.

Seconds later, they threw Thos's body into the truck.

'Something for ye shower to think on,' Kearney said, wiping his hand in his tunic sleeve.

Chalky sat dazed, shivering all over. *God, this isn't happening, this isn't happening … this isn't …* The lorry lumbered over the bridge, drove past the stand at the Curragh Racecourse, down the sloping Newbridge road and then branched right for the Curragh Camp. The searchlight tore the night apart as it moved in great shafts of light across the plains and approach roads. A large moon face. Diesel fumes from the lorry's exhaust carried to his nostrils and soured his stomach. He tried not to look at Thos. The corpse lay on its back, arms raised a little, like he would rest them on the armrests of an easy chair. Also, in the sweep of silvery and ghostly light, he saw his face in that of Thos.

They came late afternoon, as daylight waned, the officers in their best greens and full Sam Browne belts into each individual cell, to each individual prisoner, to deliver news of the sentences. Chalky had a warning for he had heard Mangan shouting at the officers and Moore saying in a loud voice that as the column's officer he should have been allowed to break the news to his men.

'No trial, ye bastards, no court martial?' he said. 'What sort are ye?'

Loud voices quietened by the redcaps' threatening words.

When they enter his cell they do not close the door. He remains sitting on the edge of his bunk. He recognises the slightly built officer with the black moustache, the lean, hard face and cold green eyes, as Art Kearney. There is a determined set to his chin and his lips are like those that always appear to belong to prissy men. He is missing the little finger of his right hand. He removes his peak cap and looks into its basin as though it holds something of interest. He has a high forehead and thinning iron-grey hair. He thinks the other officer might be Buckley and he is a bull of a man with heavy shoulders and the look of someone who does not know how to move things quietly.

'I think you know what I've come to tell you,' Kearney says in a soft tone, fixing his eyes on Chalky.

'I have a fair idea.'

'Read it for him, Buckley, so that he has more than a fair idea.'

He holds a ream of paper and puts a page to the back before he begins, 'You are Stephen Martin White, of Cross Cottages, Kildare town?'

'Yes.'

'You, Stephen White, have been charged by a military committee of being in possession, without proper authority, of ten rifles, two hundred rounds of ammunition, four bomb detonators and one exploder. The penalty for this, for not availing of the weapons amnesty offered you by the provisional government, is death by firing squad. This will take place at 08:30 hours on the morning of the nineteenth of December 1922.'

Buckley's voice had been strong and unwavering. Kearney went to the window, hands behind his back.

'Do you understand what you have been told?'

'Yes.'

'I'm sorry it has to be like this.' Said quietly but without a smidgen of sincerity.

'But 'tis your own fault,' Buckley says.

'Can I ask a question?' Chalky says.

'No, you can't.' Buckley says. Kearney cants his

head as though weighing a thought and glances at Buckley, tugs at his ear lobe. It is, Chalky thinks, an unusually long ear lobe.

'Hmm, let's hear the lad out.'

'I wasn't brought in front of any military committee.'

Kearney says, 'I'm aware of that, and it's a trivial question that I'll answer with a more substantive one – you were aware of the amnesty on offer. You had the opportunity to hand in your rifle and were aware of the consequences if you didn't. Isn't that so?'

Chalky thinks how clean his boots are. You could cut your throat with the shine.

'You murdered a man, a prisoner – I'm aware of that, too.'

It is Buckley who kicks at the side of his knee, driving his heel forward. Chalky lifts his leg at the last moment, avoiding the full impact.

'Buckley!' Kearney says. The other stays his hand midair and steps back to the doorway, puts his fingers down his tunic collar as though he were letting out hot air.

Art says, his slight frame guarding the doorway, 'We're part of the military committee. As for murder – the word doesn't exist when it comes to killing scum.'

Chalky has no more in him to say.

Kearney says, 'Your case was discussed at length by a committee comprised of five officers, two of whom abstained from casting their vote.'

'And we were encouraged from the very top not to adopt a lenient stance,' Buckley says.

Chalky snaps. 'This is wrong! This is—'

'If you don't mind,' Kearney says, 'we'll leave that for you to discuss with yourself.'

Buckley stands aside to allow Kearney to walk through the doorway. He goes to follow but turns and says, 'The only consolation you have is that it'll be a quick death, and that's not a bad consolation to have, so it's not.'

Then he, too, is gone. A redcap closes the door, turns the key. *So now you know for sure. Mangan was right.*

He stares ahead of him at a brick, thinks of the hand who placed it there, who laid mortar and added another brick and then another, building his cell... The hand is probably dead, unmoving, though perhaps not. It is not an impossibility for the hand to have been eighteen years old when laying these bricks, and to have lived for another sixty-five or so years, not impossible for the hand to reach its eighty-third year. Indeed for it still to be alive.

But an impossibility for me ... December nineteenth. Four nights, four mornings. Oh, Jesus. They won't go through with this. No way. The nineteenth – less than a week to Christmas. No one kills anyone with just six days left to Christmas. No one is that callous, surely. Mam, when she sees me – what she won't say ...

Consolation? To die quickly? The man's a fucking eejit – they'll be four nights and four mornings dying. How can he consider that a quick death? He shakes his head, rakes his fingers through his hair. Looks at his bitten nails, rubs his lips with the back of his hand.

Christ.

He holds his hands in front of him and watches them tremble. Tears are already falling. He is cold all over. *No, this is a scare they're givin' us. That's all.*

He recalls a history lesson in school – the Brother talking about how it was the custom in olden times for the victorious in battle to kill the leaders of the vanquished army and to enslave or free the common warrior on certain conditions.

I'm not a leader, just a common warrior.

Think of the dead man with the shattered mouth and then think of Thos with his heart gone because the pistol had been rammed into his chest and the trigger squeezed. Picture yourself like that, dead, unfeeling. One second you're breathing, the next you're not. You're not anything. His mind's eye sees the carnage.

Now, ask yourself this question, hero boy – was it worth it? No. No.

Think of what you'll never see or experience again – the feel of a football in your hands, the pointed score between the lofty posts, the jingle of coins in your pocket, the feel of a crisp note in your fingers, Anto and Seanie begging you, their big brother, to give them a loan. The touch of a warm sun on your face, the cleansing coldness of a morning's frosty air in your lungs, the taste of a pint, the warmth of your mother's eyes.

And the lie of you between Alice's skinny legs, furrowing deep inside her … by Jesus, haven't you cheated yourself out of a lot?

His cell door opens and the redcap who had given

him the rosary beads says, 'I'm sorry for your troubles, boy, and for all your mother's.'

The lump in his throat does not allow Chalky a word. A cough comes, but nothing else.

'Here, take this – don't let the rest of them lads see you crying.' Chalky accepts the clean handkerchief. 'Hang on to it, lad. Youse are allowed to spend a few minutes in Moore's cell.'

He nods, for nodding is as much as he is able at this present moment to express, and walks out onto the landing, turning left to walk down to Moore's cell at the end of the row. He is last to enter. Moore sits on his bunk, flanked by Mangan and Bagnall. Under the window stand O'Connor and Johnston. Nolan leans against the wall facing the bunk and Chalky joins him, leaning his back to the wall, his backside pinning his hands there so no one can see them shake. He shakes his head at Johnston's offer of a cigarette. The smoke stings his eyes. There is a bad taste in his mouth.

The column is to a man pasty-looking, tear-filled and downcast. A line of poetry under the window reads, *The walls are all white, the rules are all shite.*

Moore coughs to clear his throat, draws heavily on his cigarette and shoots the smoke through his nostrils. 'Okay – we've all been told the news. It's not going to be easy on any of us, but it'll pass, like everything must, and we'll just have to make the most of things and behave like true soldiers.'

Because no one else is inclined to speak, he feels compelled to talk on. 'I'll know about the order and manner of the executions in a day or so and will keep you posted.'

'Is there to be no appeal?' Nolan asks.

'I don't they think they left that avenue open for us.'

'You can write to the Governor, can't you?' Johnston says.

'It doesn't matter what we do – it's a done fact. Didn't you see it in that pair of walking bastards? We're already dead.'

Dead.

Nolan says, 'How about the young lads? For fuck's sake, Bryan, you have to try and save them....'

Chalky feels a flutter of hope rise within him.

Moore says, 'Do you think they're unaware of how young the boys are? Do you? Let me tell you something – let's have it straight out and no fairy tales – we're fucked because Thos opened his fat trap. If we'd gotten by the night without him being killed or anyone else we had some chance of saying sorry and we'd never do the likes of anything again and that sort of lark. But we're witnesses to a murder, boys – do ye not understand? A murder by a man wearing the uniform of the Free State.'

Jesus, Chalky thinks, *there* is *only the one way out of this.*

Moore goes on, 'Kearney and his henchmen are being protected by a higher authority – they're a murder squad doing the dirty deeds for politicians who are too cute to bloody their own hands.'

'Bastards,' Johnston says.

No one speaks.

'Wogan Browne ...' Mangan says into the fall of silence.

No one says a word. Moore's loud and long sigh and the soft slap of his hands against his thighs is informative enough.

Chalky says into the silence, 'That's it then.'

Again, there is silence. *That's it then.*

Breege

I watch Chalky hurry down the road and turn left, his torso leaning forward as he goes uphill, passing the church, its spear railings and statues of the Crucifixion at a corner prayer station. His hands are deep in his coat pockets and he doesn't bless himself going by the church, which isn't at all like him. I gather then that he must be sorely preoccupied; he no more wants to be going out with the lads than I want his lazy father to be out of his grave and sitting in the armchair spouting his nonsense. Chalky is not a religious boy, but he would always bless himself while going by a church or a graveyard out of respect to the souls lying therein. He would also do it for luck and in the hope that he would receive a blessing.

Going to see your woman, too – the Donovan one. When Sheila next door brought me the rumour in the afternoon, I waited for a smile to break out on her chubby face. But 'twas true. I tell you, a town has small pockets and no coin in them can touch off another without the rest knowing.

What can I say to a lad who is eighteen and able to fire a gun and wants to go killing people? Not a thing. You could be Solomon himself dispensing wisdom and all he'd hear from Chalky in response is 'I have to' or 'The lads are depending on me' or 'I'm a soldier' and 'Collins had no right to let go of the North.'

As for herself ... Miss D. She is, after all, a very pretty woman and has held onto her figure and so I can see why any man would be tempted. But Chalky's a mere boy and she isn't too far under forty, if she hasn't already reached it. And the names of the men associated with her down the years make for long reading, so Sheila says. You do have to be careful with Sheila Aiken and take what she says with a grain of salt, for she is horrid jealous of anyone who has more than her, including any woman with a good figure and a sweet face. It's part of her nature to begrudge and what bad she says of people she'd say of me if she thought I'd a shilling more than her. Her husband, Eddie, is one of those men you won't squeeze a word out of unless he's drunk. Then you'd hear the gombeen talk, if it's proper to call talking through his arse talking. And a singer too, I might add – he sings hymns at funerals. If it wasn't so serious it'd be hilarious. He does outcroak the crows.

It's dark. Cold, too. Icy. I can't see him now. He must be halfway up Bride Street, crossing the road to Market Square and down Nugent Street, heading for wherever it is that he meets with his friends. Tell you nothing, Chalky. So unlike the boy who used to tell me everything.

A slight breeze is on the rise and stirs the conifers across the road. I look up at the stars and think of the blood-red moon I'd allowed Chalky stay up and watch when he was small. Sonny said it was a portent of things to come. He wouldn't get off his behind and come outside and watch the lunar eclipse with us. Said he was too tired – he'd been on his feet all day.

'Sonny White,' I said, 'you see bad in everything and everyone.'

'I do,' he said, proceeding to cough his heart up.

Reluctantly, as though the moment might dissolve something irretrievable – I suppose by remaining at the gate I am trying to hold onto the tailcoat of time, to slow its advance – I turn and walk down the gravel path to the front door, press down on the latch and go in.

A sour feeling lies in the pit of my stomach. Like bad milk in tea. Anto and Seanie are toasting bread in front of the fire. Anto is fourteen and Seanie is twelve. Truth be known, Seanie is Wilson's … but the truth of it is known only to the town's mathematicians, its hoarders of other people's failings and the parish priest, Father Peter Swan, who is tied by Canon Law to keeping what he knows to himself. He is a cantankerous oul' lad with a face as sharp as any cutting wind. He used to stop and talk to me all the time before I told him my sin and now he walks by me with his nose in the air. Throwing who I am and what I'd done into my face. As if he is sinless – one day I will tell him that I know different and waylay him with news he thinks no one knows of, or if they are aware, would be too afraid to say.

I think whatever male company a widow keeps is a widow's business. But I wasn't a widow when Wilson started putting it in me – but I'm only human and sure, the honey in my marriage had long run out and for a long while Sonny wouldn't touch me and then he couldn't because he was spent in that way. A woman has needs like those of a man, which is a surprise to some people, though why that should be the case continues to intrigue me. So I have no axe to grind with Alice Donovan. I'm not a person who'd berate a person for falling off a pedestal, having done so myself. But there are some who would, and what they're doing is really berating themselves.

Anto, wiry boy, not going to be tall, says, 'Mam, is Chalky coming home tonight?'

'No.'

'Why not?' Seanie asks, going to be stocky like his father and practical too.

'He has business to look after.'

'Wilson says he's stone hammered mad for fighting against the odds,' Anto says.

'Wilson is right,' I say.

'Yes – it's like trying to take on four boys by yourself in the schoolyard, isn't it, Mam?' Seanie says.

'Exactly,' I say.

'Hmm,' Anto says. 'When are we going to get electrified? The Dunnes have a light bulb in their house – you just turn on a switch in the wall and hey presto!'

'Maybe next year.'

'Everything is next year with us,' Anto says.

'Boys, you're going to burn your toast.'

In bed, Anto is reading one of Chalky's old books, *Black Beauty*. He is struggling to keep his eyes open. He has tousled brown hair and in the light of the oil lamp he appears more innocent than he is in daylight. I suppose we all look better in half-light. More vulnerable, too. His shadow is on the wall and the sash window is raised just a little, enough for the breeze to stir the net curtain and the floral curtains I have yet to draw. Seanie is asleep, lying on his side with his back to me, the blankets off his bare skinny shoulders.

'Mam?' Anto says, voice full of sleepiness.

'Yes?'

'Do you think if I asked him that Chalky would let me fire his rifle?'

I resist the urge to cuff his ear. 'Having one lead drum in the house is enough. I don't need you to get involved in that carry-on too.' I close the window and draw the curtains. I think he knows by my exaggerated actions that he is treading dangerous ground. 'Now, it's late – go to sleep. You've school in the morning.'

I blow out the lamp and kill his shadow. I hear him close his book and let it fall on to his bedside rug. A Chalky habit, too.

Deep sleep … so deep.

Surfacing now, but I don't want to leave it behind because nothing can touch me when I am deep and oh so pleasurably lost to the world. Some nights I can't get to sleep at all. A few nights I find it after a while spent tossing and turning. Then there are nights when I climb into bed after getting off my knees, prayers finished, and catch it as soon as my head touches the pillow. It shouldn't have been like that tonight, for I was deeply troubled, but it was, and I went into a deep sleep. I suppose it was because I'd told myself that I'd get up in a minute and make tea, do a bit of ironing, wait the night out and see what the morning brings; Wilson maintains that there's such a thing as striving too hard to obtain our heart's wish. He said that if he put a few bob on a horse when he badly needed it to win, it invariably lost; his wins appear to happen whenever he isn't in dire need of the money. Grinning, he went on, 'That's why my wins are so rare.'

I am awake, still muzzy headed from coming to the surface too quickly. The knocking on the front door, the scattering of stones against my bedroom window like a dash of errant hail. The loud whispery call of my name. Again.

In the middle of the night.

When Chalky's face steals into my mind, a little beat of gladness fills me. He's home, done with all his fighting and all his carousing.

'I'm coming! Will you hold onto your horses,' I say, not bothering to cover my feet against the cold bare wood of the stairs and floor.

'Mam?' Anto says from his bedroom.

'Shush, Anto – go back to sleep.'

Again, the knocking, again the whisper. 'Breege?'

I open the door wide. 'Sheila?' Her hands are clasped to her face, pushed-up cheeks closing her eyes to slits.

'They got them, they got them last night – out in Moore's Bridge. Eddie was in the pub when the news came in. A couple of the soldiers were talking about it. They said Thos Behan got the works.'

'Merciful Jesus,' I say.

I step back inside, thinking a multitude of things as Sheila goes and fusses with stoking the fire and bringing the kettle to the boil to make a hot drop of tea.

'Did Eddie say anything else?' I ask, feeling numb inside. All the warmth has abandoned me, fled from my bones. I pick up a woollen shawl and put it round my shoulders. For no reason I think of what Wilson said to me the other day: 'There's less of you in the mirror these days.' Meaning that the weight was falling off me. He's right, and I am sure it has to do with the ball of tension in my lower belly and the fact that my appetite is not what it was.

'No, I sent him down to the house of one of the soldiers to find out more. He knows the lad's father well. He'll bring us back more news.'

'I don't think this involves my Chalky – he was going off with your woman Donovan tonight.'

'Let's hope he's with her and not with the boys,' she says.

Yesterday, Sheila wanted to know what I was going to do about the Donovan hoor getting her claws into Chalky. Immoral slut, she'd said. *Really?* I'd thought, wondering to myself what she said behind my back concerning Wilson and me. A pity of it that he isn't with me – he'd know what to do. He has a head able to suss out what needs doing in any given situation. His brother Malachy is on his deathbed the far side of the town, in his cottage on Dunmurry Hill. An old boy of 76.

She hands me a mug of tea and sits across from me on the opposite little bench flanking the fire. Black runs of paint on it where Chalky had been in a hurry and careless as a consequence.

'Will we say a Hail Mary?' she says, taking rosary beads from her apron pocket. So we say a Hail Mary. We say three, one after the other, and then we sip at our tea. She always makes it too strong but I think strong tea is what I need right now.

Eddie has further news, but it tells us nothing of importance; the soldier's oul' fella and he don't get on and the young fella isn't approachable when he has drink coursing through his veins. His mother refused to act as intermediary, saying the cur would give her nothing only the height of lip. Best to try again in the morning, after he'd eaten breakfast – he was off until late afternoon. Though, she warned, when sober he wasn't given to saying a whole lot about what went on in the Curragh Camp.

'Not much good, that,' Sheila says after seeing Eddie out the door.

'I'll go see Kevin at the station when it opens,' I say.

I leave Sheila in charge of two households and walk to the station to see Kevin Heffernan to ask if he'd heard any word about his lads who work on the lines. Chalky is a house painter amongst other things, but he'd done precious little of anything since becoming involved in the war. He'd wanted a job at the station to be with his pals, but Kevin said he already had enough troublemakers.

The platforms are empty. There is no one in the ticket office. It's early, shortly after 7 o'clock.

I hear him whistling as he passes in under the archway. When he turns into the corridor and sees me waiting at the ticket window, the whistling dies on his lips. We know each other to see.

'I take it you've heard the bad news, Mrs White?' he says, jingling a bunch of keys in his wart-bothered hand.

'Bad news and you the happy whistler?'

He adjusts his half-moon spectacles, though the action is completely unnecessary. His bushy eyebrows sink toward each other. He looks down at the lock in the grey door, fits and turns a key, then faces me. He has hollow cheeks and brilliantined ginger hair. A little lump of a stomach on the otherwise thin man.

'It's not bad news for me, I'll admit.' He steps into the office and says, 'Come ahead – there's no heat to be had standing outside.'

He takes a poker from a stand beside the potbelly stove and works on the fire kept going through the night by a night watchman. There's a fine film of dust on the turf in the wicker basket and the smells of grease and oil are potent. A wall calendar showing the month of December is smeared with grime. Nest of fag butts in a glass ashtray and green mould in the dregs of tea left in tin mugs on a counter.

'So?' I say.

'Jimmy Mangan up the road from me said the boys were caught yesterday evening and locked up in the Glasshouse. And that Thos Behan had been shot dead while attempting to escape.' He smiles what I think is an inappropriate smile and continues, 'That was Thos for you. It brought a smart end to his cheek and divilment.'

I feel like breaking his face. I'd met Thos Behan only the twice and he seemed like a nice man and I reminded him of his promise to take good care of Chalky and he said he was minding him like he was his own son. A couple of days ago he gave Chalky some chocolates to give me, handmade, and the week before he sent in a bottle of port when he heard I had a heavy cold. There was a bit of nature in the man, and clever too; I could see why he was an officer. Ah sure, he was decent. God be good to him …

'What's going to happen to them?' I ask.

The question wipes the smile from his face. He holds out his hands in a gesture of helplessness and sighs, 'I haven't allowed myself to dwell on the consequences of their being apprehended. The mood is bad against them and the war – there's the dirtiest of deeds being perpetrated by both sides.'

'They won't …'

'What – execute them? Hardly not, no – I doubt if they'll do that. But,' he looks at me over the horizon of his spectacles, 'they *could* very well do that.'

Kevin offers me tea, but I think of the mould in the mugs and besides, I don't really want to linger for too long in the company of someone who is not very good at hiding his true feelings about the column's predicament. He is, after all, the happy whistler.

Daylight is sieving through the heavens as I step outside the station. A train sounds in the distance, from the west. A bitter wind rustles bronze and yellowy leaves in and around a shore – a perforated drainpipe leans away from the brickwork, straining against its bracket, spiral of the screws visible, slowly losing their purchase.

The Stationmaster's house … there's a certain sag about the place since his wife Moira died. House dying, Kevin thriving … the merry widower searching for another wife. In his favour, a house and respectable earnings, but a woman would want to ignore a lot of bad about him for the sake of those things. I consider walking over the bridge to see the Johnstons and Nolans, who live on the Rathbride road. Might do no harm at all to walk the couple of miles to Father Moore's well on the Milltown road and say a novena.

The last one I said, along with blessing him with the holy water, cured Anto of ringworm. But the days when I could walk for miles without it leaving a strain are behind me. There's a vein as wide as a river in the back of my leg and it does give me an amount of trouble whenever I walk even a short distance. Forty-one years old and complaining of aliments my mother didn't complain of until she'd reached seventy-five. I wouldn't bet on reaching my mother's age – seventy-seven she was when she passed over, God be good to her.

I head for the Mangans, who live at the foot of Chapel Hill, a hundred yards from the walls of the cathedral and the round tower. I don't particularly like Jimmy Mangan, for he's a man who if a ship were sinking would bail in water rather than out.

I turn right at the top of the road, leaving at my back a railway bridge and the road directly under it that always floods in heavy rain. The park is to my right, with its crooked goalposts. One of Chalky's favourite haunts. God, it's cold.

They're up. And why wouldn't they be? For a moment it is in me to walk on by, up the hill, to go home and see how my lads are keeping. Neither the Mangans nor the Nolans nor the Johnstons had bothered to come knocking on my door in search of what way the land lies. Why should I hammer on theirs? *Because that's how you are.* Perhaps none of their lads was caught – perhaps …?

I knock on the door. Hens cluck in the yard and

an old collie looks me up and down, the bark long dead in her, and limps along to a wooden shed. A line of washing billows in the side yard. There is grass in the thatch roof and the stubby chimney pot is cracked.

As I knock, Jimmy Mangan walks round the gable end. He wears an old trilby hat and his lean jaw carries heavy stubble. He brings his braces from his hips and lets them land with a slap on his shoulders. A ruff of thick brown hair sticks out over the top buttons of his striped cotton shirt. His features are as dark as thunder cloud.

'She won't answer,' he says in a hard way. Like her silence was my fault. 'She hasn't spoken since we got the word last night.'

'Last night?'

'Aye. Last night,' he says. 'Why, when did you hear?'

'Early this morning.'

'So bad news doesn't always travel fast. Will you come in?'

'For a minute or so, Jimmy – I need to see my lads.'

I lead the way in. Bella Mangan sits plump in a fireside chair. The kitchen is clean, spotless, as it should be when the children have grown and flown and all that's left for a couple to do is clean up after themselves.

Bella's a large woman, broad-shouldered. Her brown hair has a middle parting and falls to mid-length – she is, I notice, suddenly feeling a terrible pity for her, thinning on top. Her lips are clenched and her eyes hold the flickering blue and orange flames in the fireplace. The soul of the house is in the fire, my mother used say. When it's out, so is the soul.

'Not a fecking word out of her since we got the news,' Jimmy says.

'Bella?' I say, putting my hand on her shoulder, rocking her gently. She doesn't see me though her pale blue eyes are wide open. 'Bella?'

'It's no good,' Jimmy says. He indicates for me to sit at the table. We drink tea. He'd poured a mug for Bella but she didn't take notice of it. There's a smell of head sweat from his hat that he's placed close to his elbow. His hazel eyes are round, close together and deep set. I'm not surprised that he sees so very little, seeing as his eyes peer at the world from so far back.

'Things are not looking good for them,' he says.

This comes out of him every second sentence and I say, 'Hold on there, Jimmy, but do you know what? You'd make for a bad undertaker, for you'd bury the dying before their last breath gave out on them.'

He speaks through his teeth. 'It's the truth of it – they're fucked.'

I remain silent, looking at him over the brim of my mug.

'Who brought you the news?' I ask.

'Maggie Johnston. She picked it up from one of the lads who went out to Moore's Bridge late yesterday evening. There wasn't a shadow left in the place. The homestead was wrecked, blood everywhere.'

'Does she know how many of them were …?'

'The lot – anyone who was there was lifted. The woman and her daughters, too.'

'Nora?'

'They put a bayonet in the dog's throat.'

'Jesus.'

'Aye, a bayonet.'

I cross myself. 'Thos ...?' I ask, though I already know his fate.

'He's dead. I don't know how or what the circumstances were.'

I still don't know if Chalky is among the captured. I could find out fast enough by paying Alice Donovan a visit, but I'm delaying doing that because if he's not with her then I know for sure where he is. And I do not want to know that for sure. *He is with her. He is.*

'So what will you do, Jimmy?'

'I'm going to the Camp later on, as soon as Nora's sister gets here. I wish to blazes she'd hurry herself on. I can't up out of the house the way she is – the doctor's coming in the afternoon.'

'If you hear anything ...'

'I'll let you know. You can come with me if you like.'

He's not there.

'No, maybe tomorrow. I'll get Wilson to bring me out.'

'I hear Malachy won't see out the week.'

'No ... so the doctor says.'

'He's been saying that about him for weeks, though, hasn't he?'

'Yes, he has.'

Without warning, he reaches out and covers my

hand with his. 'Breege, I've a horrid rotten feeling in my gut about all of this. I know you think I'm always looking at the black side of things, but Jesus Christ, I … I …'

I am aware that he's staring at me, but I can't bring myself to meet his gaze, to bring on board his wild fear. What's in my eyes takes a step back.

I leave Jimmy Mangan at his door and walk up Chapel Hill and round by Firehouse Lane, leading to the marketplace. The tall cathedral walls are ivy-covered and bending inwards in parts. When I was a child, I'd never walk close to the wall in case it collapsed on me, and I used marvel at people who lived in houses under the round tower, how they slept at night in high winds that might topple the tower down on them. Childish fears soothed only a little by my mother, who said if the tower hadn't fallen on anyone in a thousand years, it was hardly going to do so now. Missing the point entirely – it was *because* it was so old that it could fall at any moment.

For a few moments, I walk as close to the wall as possible.

The house is empty and I hate its emptiness. What is a house without a heart beating in it? Nothing; only a shell. My mother's dresser with pieces of Wedgwood delft and burn marks left by hot ash fallen from my father's pipe. On the wall the photograph of the market square, taken at the turn of the century, the shoeless boy about to cross the road, the donkey and cart, the market-square building – nothing much has changed in twenty-two years, except the people in it are that much older or dead.

I walk out into the backyard and call Sheila. The hedging is tall and dense, so I don't see her when she comes out.

She says she'll send the boys in right away and asks in the next breath, 'Any news?'

'No, Sheila – no news.'

'No news is good news.'

Is it? I ask myself. Anto and Seanie fret about Chalky and ask twenty questions at a time until I shout at them to stop. But they keep going.

'Where's Chalky?'

'When is he coming home?'

'Is Chalky in trouble?'

'Chalky said he'd bring me to the park.'

'Chalky promised me sweets and lemonade.'

On and on till I shriek, *'Stop!'*

And the shriek in me is nothing like they'd ever heard out of me before, so they stop flapping their lips immediately. The whole house, I think, is about to shake with the silence.

An hour later, the whole business is gnawing wildly at my insides. I sit at the table pushing rosary beads along thumb and forefinger. The boys and I have just finished reciting a decade of the rosary, and they'd gone outside to play in case I start the praying again.

When I hear Wilson arrive in his donkey and cart, I hurry outside to meet him before he tethers up. He hasn't touched his foot to the ground.

'I need you to bring me someplace.'

'Now?' he says. He's grim-faced. Bars of wrinkles stand upright along his upper lip. He looks at me and nods and says, 'Where?'

'To see the Donovan woman.'

'Okay, Breege.' He has the cut about him of someone who hasn't eaten or slept.

In the height of my troubles, I forgot that he has his own share. 'Malachy?' I say.

'He went early this morning.'

Of all his other brothers, he was fondest of Malachy. I feel bad in myself for not asking him straight off about his brother. After all, his face had been hanging longer than usual, his greeting uttered in as low a voice as I'd ever heard him speak. Blinded by my own troubles, I was. I say this to him and add, rubbing the back of his hand, 'I'm sorry for your loss.'

'Comes to us all, I suppose.'

He eats a spoonful of porridge, no more. Sips a sup of tea, no more. And says with a degree of frustration at not being able to still himself for a few minutes, 'We should make a move, Breege, I have things to do.'

We ride down the mile and a bit in his cart, drawn by Teddy, his little grey donkey.

She is surprised to see me and so too are her aged parents. They look at me as I look over the half-door at them at their table. They're enjoying scrambled egg and toast.

There's a surge of disappointment in me – *he is not with her*. Yet she's hardly going to parade him in front of her parents, is she? I wait for an invitation to enter, but it isn't forthcoming. I must have no mouth on me to drink their tea.

I say, 'Can I have a word with you, Alice, a moment?'

And still they don't invite me in, which I think is highly ignorant of them – I wouldn't leave a leper standing on the doormat. All you can do with some aspects of ignorance is tell yourself that some people know no better. They're beyond educating.

She walks me to the red wicket gate at the front garden, out of earshot, and says, 'What's the matter, Mrs White?'

'What's the matter?' I say to a woman about four or five years younger than me. A thought that disquiets. She could well be a sister, Chalky's aunt.

'Yes,' she says in a tone that gives me a glimpse of her inner steel.

'Where is he?' A stupid question, as I'd already half-guessed by her expression upon seeing me that Chalky had not been with her last night. My question is borne out of forlorn hope.

'I don't know, Mrs White.'

'Well, then, I know where he is now, for definite.'

'Has something happened to him?'

I tell her all and she shades very pale and I can see she has feelings for Chalky, at the very least, a fledgling love for him. Either that, or a pity, a wish in her to love some man who might want more than her flesh.

'I knew it,' she says and shakes her head. Her eyes fill and not wanting to shed tears in front of a stranger or her own family, she opens the red gate and passes through it, hurrying across the road to a wooden stile in a low whitewashed wall. Beyond lies a small wood that I'd only ever been in once and that was with Sonny, the first time he went searching through me with his bony fingers.

Seems a long time ago …

On the way back, beginning the journey, I say, 'He's in the Glasshouse.'

Wilson says nothing. I suspect he would like to say something, to call Chalky a fool, an eejit. But I might be just thinking that of him and in truth he might not want to say any such thing.

Wilson says, 'I want to call in to Father Swan and make the funeral arrangements.'

A thought occurs to me and I say, 'When you're done talking to him, you might ask him if I can have a word?'

'Sure, why don't you come in with me?'

'No. It wouldn't be right, the two of us in front of a priest.'

'Sure, you're a widow and—'

'No.'

'I see,' he says. 'Giddy up there, Teddy.'

He's a little put out that I didn't explain to him in

detail the reason for not seeing the priest. I'd confessed to Father Swan about my adultery and the reaction I got from him was not the one I'd been expecting. He'd pegged a number of prayers my way as penance and told me not to sin again – but he didn't leave my sins in the confessional. He brought them around with him and threw them at me with his eyes every time our paths crossed. Tell Wilson?

Why should a woman have to spend her life confessing to men? They can go to blazes, the lot of them.

He ties Teddy's reins to a black wall ring inside the grounds of the parochial house. You could fit four or five large families in a house that size and they wouldn't get in each other's way. It has the sombreness of a place lived in by a host of bachelors. If it wouldn't get their cleaning and cooking lady, Stella Devine, in trouble, I'd waylay into Father Peter about the nights he falls into bed drunk and of the time he put a hand on Stella's thigh.

She told me, 'Up his hand came, like a frog hopping along my leg. "Fadder," I sez, "where are you going with that hand and I in the rags?"'

And Stella is not one to lie – or lie with men. It's her hope to die a virgin. There are times when I think she's the wisest woman I know. Wilson has a hump with me and doesn't say a word before setting off across the stony path to the back door. He has a cigarette in his mouth and he walks in a way that he doesn't normally; he is leaning forward in himself, ready to bow, if you ask me.

The men other men bow to, I ask you.

I step down from the cart and walk around the yard, bursting for a piddle but nowhere to do it, unless I go in and ask Stella if I can use the bathroom. But I don't want your man to know that Stella and I are friends. He might make life awkward for her – if he hasn't already, that is. There's the outhouse, but the smell of it – sure, I wouldn't let Teddy piddle in it, not even from outside. Have to hold on.

The sun shines through the beech trees, but there's no warmth, it gets colder when the sun goes behind cloud.

Wilson emerges a few minutes later. We meet in the shadow of the beeches. He has his cap on and his back is straight, rid of the subservient appearance.

'He didn't keep you too long,' I say.

'He'll keep you less – he's too busy to see you.'

'Is he now?'

'Breege …' He grips my elbow as I go to pass him by and I shake it free and say, 'Don't, Wilson – don't ever do that.'

I push the green back door, down the tiled hallway, and into the study. Father Peter is sitting behind a large desk. He's an avuncular-looking man with a small mouth. Hairs protrude from his ears and his nostrils, like weeds you'd see in garden baskets.

'Father.'

He looks up at me. Through me, too. I tell you, his eyes have stripped many women bare.

'I'm very busy,' he says, lowering his gaze.

Be nice. Be subservient. 'What I have to say won't delay you too long, Father.'

He pinches his nose between his thumb and forefinger and sighs. 'What is it?'

I tell him about last night's business. As I speak, I wonder if he's listening. He picks up a blue fountain pen and holds it between his forefingers, his eyes fixed on its length, like he is studying its power at rest.

Finished speaking, he says, our eyes locking, 'You still haven't told me what it is you want.'

'Will you speak with the prison chaplain? I want to see Chalky, bring him—'

He waves a hand dismissively. 'Absolutely out of the question.'

'Why?'

'Why? I'll tell you why. They've robbed shops in town, bullied and intimidated the locals, fighting a war they'd no just cause for starting in the first place, causing mayhem and destruction. Is that enough for you?'

'He's only eighteen.'

'Old enough to know the difference between right and wrong.'

'A child.'

'An eighteen-year-old child. There's no such thing, woman. Now get out, will you? Just go. I have—'

'So you won't arrange things?'

'I haven't got the power to arrange anything.'

'You won't bother your barney, you mean.'

He stands to his full height, a rangy man. His priest clothes are wrinkled and around the shoulders lie spreads of dandruff.

'He and his kind come into the church, walk out during my sermon and come back in when I've finished – they know the will of their Church and they defy it. Let me remind you of young Wogan Browne last February – of the shops they raided, of the men they put revolvers to because they thought they were plainclothes police. Frightened the life out of them. Why didn't you stop your boy's gallivanting? And now, now you ask me to help them.'

'It'd be Christian of you.'

His words come in a rush. 'Out, now!'

'I'm going. But let me tell you this – you're no good – no good. Without that collar round your neck, you'd be nothing.'

There's a fall into near silence, the only noise that of his breathing coming through his hairy nostrils, like a bellows too old and in bad repair.

When he speaks, there is almost a shiny gloat in his eyes. 'We are looking forward to having our town back and peace and prosperity now that its streets have been cleaned of dirt.'

It's in me to spit at him, but something holds me back. I hope he dies roaring.

He looks behind me at the door. 'Now go before I take a whip to you. Stella!'

'A whip?' I say. The pup.

I am not aware that the door had opened nor of Stella's presence. I catch sight of her in the corner of my eye. She has this shocked expression on her face – she's never heard anyone speak so insolently to a man of the cloth.

'See this yoke out,' the priest says.

I hurry out and the anger in me burns so strongly that I walk by Wilson and ignore him. And I keep walking, refusing to listen to him calling my name. A bully priest and a wimp of a man. Gobshites.

I have a picture of Chalky in my head, languishing in a prison cell. He's not one for being able to stick being fettered to the one spot. It'll play on his mind. Three days now and not an official word from the authorities about the lads, how they were caught, what they were caught doing and, more importantly, what they intend doing with them.

I mix and match what I know with the rumours Sheila and others have come back to me with. *I know* that there was a weapons amnesty offered by the provisional government and that anyone after a specific date who was found to be in possession of a firearm and ammunition would be executed.

I know that the specific date has long gone by, ignored by the column. *I know* that there are internment camps of wooden huts close to the Glasshouse and that the Glasshouse is a stone and brick prison with a glass roof and is the punishment centre for the Irregulars, those the authorities regard as 'trenchant republicans'.

I think that means unrepentant.

Rumours …

They tell me that there is no hope for the boys.

That soldiers in pubs and at checkpoints have told people the lads were rightly fucked. That Thos Behan was shot in cold blood by one of his *own* men. That Thos Behan was beaten to death. That Thos Behan is not dead but badly wounded.

I keep a candle going in the kitchen, on the ledge of the dresser, and have beaten a path to the Carmelite Church that is situated at the mouth of the old Rathangan road that leads to Thos Behan's village. The fact that a woman with bad legs should walk past one church a hundred yards from her front door and go to another should say enough to people, if they cared to listen, about what this woman thought of the love, kindness and forgiveness she could expect to find within the hallowed walls of the nearest. The friars are pleasant but they're not the ones with influence and when I asked Father Tony if there was any way he could help, he said he would make a call, and he did, but when he came back into the kitchen where I was drinking tea with Mrs Hannifan, his cleaning lady, he shook his head and said, 'They're not even willing to discuss the subject with me, Breege. I'm sorry.'

I didn't ask who he had called. I presumed it was someone high up in the army or the Curragh.

The mood in town has changed – there's something in the air, an expectancy. There are those who have commiserated with me and those who have not, who ignore me as they always did, seeing nothing in me that would do for them. The mood is strange.

It is like me and my boys are being held responsible

for all that had gone on in the town. Like we are to blame because we didn't try to prevent his antics or weren't a good enough reason for Chalky to give up the business he was in. I'm not stupid or blind. They blame, and they enjoy their blaming.

Though it is only three days since their arrest, the absence of the column in the town is one of relief for the counter men. They can go around and do their business without the fear of young scuts coming in and robbing them blind at gunpoint.

But can they not see that I'm his mother and what good is a woman if she doesn't have the human nature to stand by those she brings into the world? What would they have their own mothers do if they found themselves in the same situation as my Chalky?

How could I stop my Chalky fighting for what he believed in when I believe in the same cause – a free Ireland, all of it free, and not a corner of it lent to the Crown as Collins tried to dupe us into believing? He's dead now, but he'd done the harm before he went – the good and the harm of it – and yet Chalky revered him. Like his father. Now there was a waster if ever there was one – the great Sonny - great at making the speeches and firing up a young boy's imagination. Much like the Christian Brothers were for stoking up hatred of all things English and Irish men who nursed English thoughts in Gaelic hearts. Sit back then, the bastards, God forgive me, and let young men die early deaths.

Die early deaths.

The thought chills me to the marrow.

I get to my feet and blow out the guttering candle on the dresser and light another. I am worn out with all the worry and the argument with Father Swan has further tightened the knot in my stomach.

No members of the other afflicted families have called to my door. I'd expected Jimmy Mangan to visit as he said he would, but he hasn't thus far, unless I was out when he called, but I doubt if this is the case. I would say he is no wiser now than he was before he visited the Camp and simply didn't think it worth the while to bring me no fresh news.

I need to buy in some groceries and slip on my coat and scarf and count up my pennies.

I walk up the hill, my vein giving me an amount of grief but I offer it up for Chalky, so the good Lord will see him out of this mess, allow him one chance, just one.

The ground is wet from last night's heavy fall of rain and the breeze, though light, is skinning. The town is quiet.

I see Mrs Johnston – I know her as Mrs J, we were childhood friends – and she also sees me, but pretends not to. She disappears around the corner at Boland's Merchants and then doubles back. Her face is dark and I can see the hurt and anger in her.

'Come here, you,' she says to me.

Not what I had been expecting. I thought we might be kindred spirits, seeing as our loss is identical.

'Your Chalky led my fella astray and look where

he's brought him – an ill-reared little fucker, he is.'

'Look', I say, 'your lad's as old as mine and didn't need anyone to bring him anywhere. You weren't cribbing about the boys when they gave you your fancy-smelling perfume, were you, and fancy mince pies from Bewleys, were you, you smelly oul' bitch?'

She turns on her heels and walks away.

A little shakily, I cross the road, almost skidding on a pat of dung, jarring my lower back. Oh merciful Jesus, the pain, oh holy mother of God, the pinch of it. I steady myself by putting my hand on the chemist sill. In the window there's a yellowy advertisement to buy a cough elixir.

Christ, the pain.

Is that me, my reflection in the window, with the clouds blowing past over my head? Do I look that wretched? That mad?

I sweep in a breath of air and then another and walk the few steps round the corner to the vegetable man. I'd sooner shop in Dilly Dwyer's but I can't walk that far as she's down the end of Claregate Street – too much pain in me.

Louis Devine is talking away to Mrs Hennessy, who never has a kind word for man or beast, and when he sees me he turns the conversation to the boys in the Glasshouse and wonders aloud if they'll be executed.

Your woman, who hasn't seen me, who wouldn't turn her head to see who'd come into the shop because as far as she was concerned, no one more important than herself would shop there that day, says, 'Where there's life, there's hope.'

And when his eyes alert her to my presence, she almost dies, her mouth drops open and it's easy to see she is vexed with Devine for walking her into the mire. I cut her in two with a look but my tongue goes sideways in me and I can't speak. A rare thing indeed for me not to find a word.

I pay up for the cabbage and leave.

I cook a dinner in silent rage and throw the cabbage out because of the vegetable man's sneer and the bitch Hennessy's cruel words. Me and my boys won't eat a cabbage on which a man sneered and a woman dropped a hope that my son would be shot.

It is late in the afternoon when his shadow casts itself in my kitchen.

'It's you,' I say.

He is in his black suit and best shoes. 'You didn't make the funeral. I thought about—'

'I didn't. There's nothing wrong with your eyesight.'

'Malachy would have been hurt – he was fierce fond of you. But—'

'He might also understand.'

'I was about to say that.'

I do not invite him to sit. When the boys come in and fuss over him, I tell them to get out and stay out.

'You haven't calmed down any,' he remarks, watching their sullen exit, promising to catch them later – bullseyes and acid drops, hard-boiled sweets.

'I couldn't go to the funeral – not with Swan doing

the rites – and I've put my back out. Between that and my leg and the pain in my stomach, I don't know which end of me is up.'

He nods – I don't know why – perhaps in response to a self-posed question – and draws out a chair and sits to it.

'Is the tae hot?' he says.

'I doubt it, 'tis made since midday.'

'You were hard on the priest – Stella told me.'

'He threatened to whip me.'

''Tis only a saying he has, he tells everyone that when he's vexed with them. But sure, you don't see people walking around with welts, do you?'

'They're probably covered up. And shush about that fella – I don't want his name mentioned in my home.'

'Okay, Breege,' he says, holding his hands up to show he wants to placate me.

'I can do nothing for you,' I say.

'I wasn't thinking that you would.'

'I don't know if the urge will ever come to me again.'

'Sure if it doesn't, it doesn't.'

'What you'll do then?'

'Drink tae.'

I smile.

'You never called for me to see would I go to the funeral,' I say.

'Sure, I thought about asking you, but I knew you wouldn't have come and I didn't want you to feel bad about declining.'

'I wouldn't have felt badly.'

A frown darkens his features and his chin drops a little, like he is digging in for a bad reaction to whatever it is he has to tell me.

'Breege?'

'I don't want to argue—'

'Thos Behan is being waked tonight.'

The act is instinctive; I bless myself.

'At his home in Rathangan,' he says.

'I should go.'

'We both will.'

'You're very kind, Wilson.'

He drums his fingers on the table, as if there is something he needs to herald prior to announcing. 'Breege, they had a woeful job getting his body back from the army.'

'How come?'

'They were on for burying him in the Camp and not allowing the family to see the body or … The prison chaplain prevailed upon the Governor to release Thos to his family. The Governor was stood down for his trouble by his senior officers when they heard. They were hopping over it.'

Hopping, I think, *over a corpse*. Isn't it a proper dirty little war altogether?

Wilson comes into the kitchen like a rush of wind and says, 'Gerry is waiting for us; he's parked on the island.'

Meaning the triangle of space across the road from Saint Brigid's church. He has a face on him like a boy warning another about someone or something. Like it was a mortal sin to delay this man. As if owning an automobile ought to distinguish him as a man of huge importance, one too important to be kept waiting, too good to come in and sip tea while waiting for me to find something decent to wear that didn't make me resemble a raggy waif.

What Gerry is doing is obliging us, and when you're under an obligation to a person, he sometimes likes you to know it. Never mind the fact that it would be almost a sin for him to travel alone, three seats empty, when he knows others are going his way. He wants to feel appreciated and us to feel grateful.

I have organised the boys to spend the night with Sheila. It'll be dark shortly after four. We're travelling by motorcar and though it has headlights, no one wants to travel the roads at night, not with what's going on. You wouldn't know what checkpoint you could meet – army or Irregular – or those pretending to be either but who are renegades, highwaymen.

Gerry Wilson, a brother of Wilson's, is driving. It's a green roofless car that he says is a Triumph. The winter cold is made worse by the speed we're travelling, all of twenty-five miles an hour, which is quite amazing. This is my second time in a motorcar and I quite like the experience. Quicker and not as bumpy – miles and miles better than riding in a donkey and cart.

Gerry and I don't like each other. It's a natural dislike and not one born out of anything one of us did to or said about the other. Though he hasn't said anything, I am aware that he resents the way I call Wilson by his surname and not by his first, which is Pat. He might think it derogatory, perhaps the way a mistress addresses her butler. Long ago, I asked Wilson if he minded and he said he didn't, that people often called him by far worse. It's habit, a name I got used to calling him long before we came to mean anything to each other.

The engine is sluggish over the steep canal bridge that bends midway and then slopes towards Rathangan's main street. Gerry parks alongside a kerb outside a pub. The engine makes ticking noises as it cools. He straps a tarpaulin over the seats and buckles up the ties, Wilson giving him a hand.

Gerry says, 'You two go on ahead, I'm going to wet my whistle before going down. Two corpses in as many days – 'tis more than my eyes can handle.'

We walk on a bit.

'I've booked a room for us in Conlan's – a room is all I could get,' Wilson says. 'There'll be no awkward looks or questions at all.'

So he has put us in the book as Mr and Mrs. There's nothing in me to say. I feel like a night's company.

The Behans live in a two-storey house close to a fork in the road. One road brings you along the side of the canal, the other the bog road to Edenderry, passing Killinthomas Wood. I saw a painting of the wood with bluebells and wild garlic in the lounge of the Railway Hotel in Kildare and thought it was simply beautiful, one of the nicest paintings I'd ever seen, a forest floor of white and blue. That night I smelled the fragrance of the woods in a dream.

A lot of people are milling around outside the house, smoking, drinking from pint glasses. All the front doors in the street are ajar and plates of sandwiches are being passed around and women are going about with black-sided kettles of tea, refilling mugs, asking people if they are okay, to step in out of the cold if they want – it's going to be a long night.

'Go on in,' an old man says when we stop, wondering what we should do, who we should seek out.

Thos Behan in his coffin … sure, there's no peace in the man's face, not a scrap of it. The crowd in the room, filing past his coffin, his hands gripping black rosary beads, the smell of candle smoke as the bitterly cold breeze in from the road causes candles to gutter and die. Hurriedly relit.

Jasus. It brings back the memory of my own man's wake and how Chalky wouldn't let go of my hand and kept saying, 'Mammy, I'll get a job, I'll get a job, don't be worrying yourself now,' and the tears washing his little face and the sobs and heaves of his small chest as sleep overtook him at night. *Hail Mary full of grace … Murmuring song of faith. The Lord is with thee …*

The skull bandaged up and oh Jay, poor Thos, three days dead, three days since he's been minding my boy.

I put my hand on Thos's. Cold, dirt under the fingernails, pennies holding his eyes closed, strapped with a blue scarf jaw to crown to prevent his mouth from opening. The breaths of those in the queue behind me push and will me on my way. They all want their last goodbye to be done with; to have their own future a memory.

'The bastards'll pay for this,' whispers one man in the scullery.

'Bad fuckers,' said another. 'If they touch one hair on the head of the others, there'll be fucking ructions.'

A young woman as worn looking as myself hands me a mug of tea and the last sandwich on a plate.

The chat out of these men doesn't do anything to calm the disturbance in me. Since talking with Jimmy Mangan, I had caught hold of his and his wife's depression – it's like we're waiting for the worst of bad news to happen.

'Don't worry yourself, Missus, he'll be grand,' says a man with a whiskey nose.

Do I know him?

'They're being well taken care of,' says an old lad who thinks he knows everything.

'I'm telling you, they'll be back working the railway lines next week,' pipes in Mister Smug. Kevin the Stationmaster, crumb of yolk on his chin.

I say, 'Are ye listening to me? The amnesty said clearly that anyone caught in possession of arms without authority would be sentenced to death. Wasn't it in the papers? Didn't I read it? Didn't the boys tell me of it themselves? "Fuck them," the boys said, laughing it off. Aye, fuck them indeed.'

People stop talking and look at me as though to ask where I had left my wake manners. Then the chatter starts up again, slowly, ebbs like a river's mountain source.

Then Kevin speaks, at the same time picking the crumb from his chin and eating it. 'Dooley is out and young Eddie Hennigan, too.'

'Where are they?' I say. They might have news of Chalky.

'Dooley's taken the boat.'

'The boat?' I say.

'And young Hennigan, he's gone to an aunt in Mountmellick.'

'What are you telling me, Kevin?'

'It's not what I'm telling you, Breege – it's what their absence is telling you.'

Wilson comes to us, says, 'I was wondering where you'd got to.'

'I'm not staying here,' I say.

'Okay, but they're about to start saying the rosary.'

I shake my head.

'Okay. Sure.'

Out on the street, heading for the hotel, we run into Gerry. He has the mark of his motoring goggles around his eyes. Red rims.

'Where are yese off to?' he says.

'The hotel. We'll have a drink there – it's hectic in Behan's,' Wilson says.

'Bound to be, bound to be … still, we have to pay our respects, eh, no matter what?' This was his cut at me for not attending Malachy's funeral.

In bed after making love, I listen to the night song of the revellers – song of the wake, giving the spirit a good send-off. The things you think of when you're alone in yourself. Wilson has his back to me, is snoring gently. My passion, my cries had alarmed him for he had not heard me cry out like that before – to stop myself I would usually land my lips in his neck, but tonight I did not care who heard. I wanted to let go, to rid myself for a few blissful seconds of the stone that weighs heavy and cold in my heart.

Gerry cranks the engine and we get into the motorcar and set off for home in the misty rain. Gerry had said he had to leave for Dublin to take care of some business there and so we decided not to attend Thos's funeral. However, I had already made up my mind to remain in the hotel, as I simply wasn't up for facing into much. Gerry runs a drapery business in Naas – he married into money. A dour woman with a hard face, according to Wilson. His real love is his Chambers automobile, which he bought second-hand in 1915 for a couple of pounds. He likes to tell people he drives it two hundred miles a week and its seven-horsepower engine rarely gives him trouble and does forty miles to the gallon of petrol.

He drives the Triumph to give his Chambers a rest. Jesus, a two-car man – but I suppose one of anything will never be enough for some people.

About four miles outside Rathangan, we turn left at a fork junction onto a longer route to town, as the Dunmurry road is long and steep and might prove too hard on the engine. A pity, as I'd fancied seeing the Medlicott house where my mother used to work as a maid. I was in it, once – a fine big house set at the end of a gravelled avenue. I remember feeling absolutely amazed that the family had their very own cemetery. There's the rich and then there's the richer; trying to bring class to the other world, if you ask me, a difference in bone as there was in flesh.

There are sheep on the Curragh and the peaks of far-off mountains are snow-covered. My very bones are shivering, teeth chattering, even under the rug and folded tarpaulin covering me chin to toe.

It is in me to ask Gerry to drive straight on, over Moore's Bridge, to the Curragh Camp, but he's not in the mood for asking. He has been silent in an abrupt sort of way. I suppose it's because he had stayed in the room next to us and had heard my raucousness. I'd seen the two brothers speaking in the lobby shortly before breakfast, almost face to face.

'It's not right,' Gerry said.

'What's not?' I asked, joining them, catching both unawares.

'None of your concern,' Gerry said.

'Are we all right for a ride?' I said, eyes blowing hard at Gerry, who did not know where to put his pair of greys.

'Home?' I explained.

'Yes,' he said stiffly.

I see the camp's Water Tower, the bellowing vapour pluming from a steam engine's funnel as it draws carriages toward Kildare station. I pray for something to give in Gerry, for him to bring me to the Camp. But whatever is in him not to make an offer is in me not to make a request.

At the island in Kildare – I don't know why he doesn't park outside my house (perhaps it has to do with his not wanting the fuss of the boys about him and his precious vehicle) – he doesn't say a word in reply to my 'Thank you, Gerry.' He pretends to be pre-occupied with a sheaf of his automobile's papers. Wilson looks at me and nods for me to remain silent.

Jaesus, I don't know. How the blazes did I end up with a coward?

He follows me across the road. I'm melting inside with temper.

'Why is it you never stick up for me?' I say outside my gate, closing it between him and me, creating a wooden divide.

'Stick up for you? What are you talking about?'

'Don't give me that tripe.'

'Ah, ignore Gerry – he's like that with everyone.' He has this pleading face on him for me to let this go. But this is his second time.

'So, I'm everyone to you – is that it?'

He sighs long and hard. All he wants now is to crawl off and have a smoke and not be listening to me. 'Sorry,' he says. 'I'm just one for the peace – you know that, Breege.'

'Peace my arse. You either learn to stand up for me or—'

'Hold on there a second,' he says. 'You're well able to defend yourself with your tongue. You don't need me for that. I'd stand in front of you to stop anyone laying a hand on you. That's when I'd step in.'

'And I should believe that?'

'Well, ask Stella what I said to Father Peter about his taking a whip to you. I went to see him after you told me.'

'You said something to him? What did you say?'

'Sure, I had to. And what he didn't say about you – it couldn't be repeated. I said that was something I wouldn't be able to stand idly by and let happen. That he should note the advice.'

'You said that?'

'I did, as God is my judge.'

'Why didn't you tell me this sooner?'

'You'd have it 'twas only words or something and that I should have said more.'

I say nothing for a few seconds and then say, opening the gate, 'We need a drop of tea in us.'

I am hurt that Gerry did not ask me about my son in the Glasshouse. Even if you hold someone in no or low regard, it is human nature, is it not, to make a general enquiry for the sake of politeness? I am sure Wilson would have told him about the situation. Gerry has made it plain that me and mine do not matter to him.

Sheila, God be good to her, has the fire lit. I hate coming home to a dead fireplace. I did the same for her when her mother passed away and she had to spend some days in Dublin, kept the fire going so that the soul of her house did not catch cold.

Wilson lights up when he sits at the table. I add turf to the fire and then sit across from him, intending to sit for only a minute, as I want to get the lads in under my roof. Then I decide they can wait a while longer.

'I want to go to the Camp in the afternoon, Wilson.'

'I'll bring you, though I think it's futile.'

'Futile? What do you mean by that?'

'A waste of time.'

'I don't consider trying to get to see my son and bring him something decent to eat a waste of time.'

He blows out smoke and says, fingering a knot in the table, 'They don't let anyone in the internment camps have visitors.'

'This is different.'

He looks at me under those heavy brows of his. 'Why?'

His question frightens me. Indeed, why? Because my son is condemned and I won't get to see him again, that for this reason an allowance ought to be made?

Oh sweet divine Jesus, no – don't.

The mist has passed, though the day remains grey, the skies holding the rain, perhaps sleet. Chestnut race-horses on the Curragh cross the road a hundred yards in front of us, Teddy clip-clopping, blinkered from all save the stretch of road ahead of him.

Chalky loves going to the races. He used to always

go on about buying a horse, a grey one with a white patch in its forehead and two white socks. Chalky is very particular regarding some things. Not about the company he kept. Not a sign of hope in the sky. No blue.

The Camp is to our left, across the grasslands and the long tiered procession of red-brick buildings and roads. Endless chimney pots, all smoking.

Wilson points and says, 'The Glasshouse is there.'

It is the westernmost building of the camp. I see only its high grey walls and tall chimney.

My boy is in there, behind that drabness. In that dreary place.

We continue east and then at Brownstown we turn and head north, so that the side of the camp we had trotted parallel to is back to the west. Going away from a place so as to come back to it – the story of my life thus far. At the top of the hill, on the public road that divides the military camp in two, we dismount. I look about me, taking my bearings, as Wilson ties up Teddy and gives him a mouthful of hay to chew on.

I've never been this close to the Water Tower. Chalky had been here the day the Union Jack was low-ered and the tricolour raised. He arrived home in a high state of melodrama, all talk about the event, his eyes wild with excitement, his clothes sopping wet. I'd have gone with him, but the day was so bad and I thought Anto was coming down with the flu.

A sign shows me to a reception office. I take two steps down and almost immediately arrive at a counter. A redcap sitting at a desk pushes back his chair and comes over to me. He has the head of a sleveen and eyes of different colours: green, brown.

'Yes?' he says.

'My name is Breege White and I've come to visit my son.'

His eyebrows climb, like he's thinking he has a quare one here. 'Is he a serving soldier?'

'No.'

'And where is he then?'

'In the Glasshouse, I believe.'

'What's your name again?'

'Breege White. My son's name is Chalky ... Stephen White.'

He shakes his head and says he'll be back in a minute. He knocks on the door of an adjoining office and enters when told to do so. Wilson sidles up to my shoulder, blowing air into his joined hands.

'Well?' he says, shaking his hands, trying to cast off the cold.

'He's gone to see someone.'

The door opens and another redcap appears. A senior rank, I can tell. He comes to the counter and says, 'I'm sorry, Missus, they're not allowed visitors. The other families who've come have been told likewise.'

'Why not?'

'Orders.'

'Orders?' I say. 'Whose orders?'

Am I to take comfort that no other family has been

allowed in to see their man? A peculiar consolation, that.

'You can head off now, we'll be in touch – that's what I was told to tell you, Missus.'

'Can you give my son this parcel?'

'No, no parcel, not even a letter, Missus. It's not my decision.'

I go outside and after walking two steps, my knees turn to water and I nearly stumble.

'Breege,' says Wilson, 'are you okay?'

'Fine. I'm not giving up, Wilson.'

'I didn't think you would. And why would you?' He suggests we go to see the prison chaplain. 'Chance our arm, Breege, keep going until we're stopped.'

We go down a camp road in the jalopy and stop to ask a couple of soldiers where we might find the chaplain. They say they don't know. The third one we stop on the road says, 'Which one, Father Magee or Father Donnelly?'

'The prison chaplain,' I say.

'They're both that, but you'll find Father Donnelly in the officers' mess having tea – he's more approachable than Father Magee. Go in round the back of the mess and ask one of the help for the mess steward. It's the mess on the top road you're needing.'

Tea – with officers, no less.

Wilson mutters under his breath and I then I follow the track of his eyes and see why he'd cursed. The redcaps have a barrier across the road. There's a corrugated hut to the side of it, smoke piling through a tin chimney with a conical cap. Wilson pulls up short of the red and white boom. Three redcaps emerge from the hut to join the other on the road. A skinny NCO walks towards us and when close up he stares at Wilson, like he is trying to match his face with a name.

'Can I see your camp pass, Mister?' the corporal says.

'I have none,' Wilson says.

'And where are you going?'

'To see Father Donnelly in the officers' mess.'

I hear the bike behind me and turn round. The sleveen eyes me hard, brakes squeaking, and says something, covering his mouth, to a sergeant, who nods and seems to say something like, 'Is that so?'

He comes over and stands at the corporal's shoulder, a big man with a heavy bottom lip. He says in a soft, flat Midland accent, 'Offa with youse pair now.'

Wilson says, 'Ah, now—'

'No "ah now" outta you. Do you want a taste of life in the internment camp? And do you, Missus, want to see the inside of Mountjoy?'

Coming to his shoulder, the sleveen says, 'Would you like that, Missus?'

'Your mother reared little,' I say.

'And you less,' he says.

I spit at him and he goes for me, but his sergeant stretches his arm out across the sleveen's little chest and says, 'Go home, Missus – go home.'

I know what else he is saying: *Go home, Missus, and wait.*

And wait …

106

Father Pat

Mrs Caulfield enters the study, squints and says, 'Father, your breakfast is ready.'

'Thank you, Maura, I'll be there in a minute.'

He is distant, reflecting on last night and the hard words he had spoken. Pity of it he had brandy taken, for he can imagine what the chat will be like at the officers' table this morning: 'Can't hold his tongue when he has drink in him.'

He would have said what he had to say without the liquor in him.

Why didn't you?

Because the evening had been cordial until a specific moment …

He does not fit in with the officer class. *How could I*, he thinks, *when I'm not of their kind?* Educated as well as any of them, thanks to the seminary in Maynooth and a spinster aunt who sponsored him on his quest to become a priest. Forgiver of sins, a lighted way for spirit, envoy of Christ …

He came from a poor background and was reared in a tenement home by a mother who had spurned her family to marry a man who promised her the stars and brought her nothing, only pain, sorrow and early widowhood. For a woman used to her comforts – well, he thinks, trying not to think too unkindly of the dead – love must be well and truly blind. His memories of his father are of his constant comings and goings, and then a final going. Dead or alive? He does not know or care – it was rumoured that he took the boat to Liverpool in pursuit of a woman and some other dream.

Good riddance to bad rubbish, his mother said, long worn of him and lately of life.

He is a well-built man of forty-nine, sliding towards corpulence, as seems to be the course for the men of his people.

He looks out through the window at a platoon of men drilling on the parade square in MacDonagh Barracks, called after one of the signatories of the 1916 Proclamation who was later executed. An act of folly that propagated the War of Independence and had led to this bloody fiasco of a civil war. A year ago the barracks was called Gough Barracks.

A year can see in a mighty degree of change.

So can a day.

A second, even.

The men on the square are recruits and out of step. The sergeant shouts 'Stad' and the recruits stagger and stumble to a halt, colliding with each other. The sergeant, a fine cross-country runner in his prime, demonstrates how to get back into step when out of it, a little kick of the right toe to the left heel. A silly dance.

'Pick up the step and keep it! Listen in – Meitheal, do rear clay. Clay, dheas, clay, dheas …'

He sighs, pushes back his chair and gets to his feet, uncomfortably aware of his burgeoning stomach and the shrinking waistline of his trousers, waist button open. During the ritual of shaving, he had looked at the wrinkles under his eyes, how deep and thickly cut they were, making his blue eyes appear smaller, the two chins and fleshy cheeks, and yet he still did not feel old inside or fat, as he no doubt is. The eyes – a pair of deceivers at times, so much so that the heart cannot depend on them. The ears perhaps even less reliable, as they sometimes hear only what it is they want to hear.

A fine one to be telling the flock to fast during Lent – what must they think while looking up at him in the pulpit?

A bit of fasting wouldn't do yourself any harm, Father.
The size of him telling us to do without, eh?

There are good reasons for dying in your prime and not in your decline. A load of bull, he tells himself.

Is it? Well, you better be lying about it, so. There are men depending on you to lie. You'll have to tell them it's a noble thing to die in your prime – except for three or four of them at least, as they're neither next nor near their prime. How'll you manage to convince them of the nobility of an early death, eh? *Buachaill …*

The dining room fire is lit and he stands in front of the red coals for a few moments and then turns his backside to the heat, staying there till he smells the fabric in his black trousers at a point of incipient scorching. He moves to the walnut table.

Fond of your food, always were. Not that you could always get it.

How many more breakfasts have you left to get in you? More than a few, more than three or four, like what's left for those poor fools in the Glasshouse.

Father Kevin Magee enters, trying to keep the argument they'd had last night from showing in his features.

No hard feelings.

Ah – there's a strain in his face from pretending that he isn't bothered. As a boy, he must never have got away with fibbing to his mother. He is a slight man with a lean face and though in his seventy-fifth year, he would pass for a man of sixty. He walks with a ramrod-straight back and sees things in black and white, as though these were the only pair of colours God gave to every situation. 'Good morning, Kevin,' he says in a conciliatory tone.

'Pat. 'Tis not a bad one at all.' Father Kevin sniffs the air. 'Is something burning?'

'My backside – I was warming the seat of my pants a few moments ago.'

'Well, it's a better smell than the one of sulphur we had to endure last night.'

'I only said what needed saying.'

A deep frown develops between the older man's eyebrows, so deep you could lose a secret in there, or two. Pat helps himself to a slice of toast from the rack and butters it, pours his tea, cracks his boiled egg. God almighty, why doesn't that woman use a strainer for the tea? She can't be that bloody forgetful, he thinks. If I could walk, if the soles of my feet and the knees didn't cause me pain after the walking, I might have some chance of losing a bit of the weight.

'About last night, Pat …' Kevin begins, sentence left trailing, saying sorry without actually having to say the word because he believes he isn't the only one who should be regretting the matter.

'Errah, Kevin, we had too much wine and the hot stuff, and we shouldn't have ended up discussing what was a discussion for the two of us alone.'

They had argued with each other in the officers' mess, and with officers too. Well, he with the officers, as Kevin had sided with them. A shower of fucking gets, the lot of them, God forgive me for saying so about an army marching in the shine of Our Lady's halo, according to the bishop.

'It's true for you, Pat – we should have kept our opposing views for the study.'

Pat sips at his tea from a red-rimmed cup. Through the bay windows steals in the faint, indistinct orders from the parade square and the sound of a breeze beginning to rise.

'Kearney most of all was unhappy with you, Pat. Do you know that? He took high offence with you.'

'I do not like that man.'

'He and that fella Buckley have a hard job.'

'They make it hard.'

'If the country didn't have men like them prepared to do the dirty work, it would be in a worse state than it is now.'

'Do you think?'

'De Valera and his crowd would have us back to square one fighting the English, losing the twenty-six counties it took us eight hundred years to win back.'

'We shouldn't be executing our own, save if it can be proven without doubt that they willingly killed another.'

'Our own? Listen to the drilling outside – they're our own, Pat, if we have to refer to any side as being ours.'

'They say Kearney has murdered—'

'Who says?'

A soldier in the confessional, Kevin, bawling his eyes out, but sure I can't tell you that. Secret of the confessional – a pair of men in a coffin with a grille between them, mincing words, truths and salvation.

'There's murder on both sides. It's down to us to do the praying and the blessing and give the last rites. Like the bishop said.'

'I don't believe in this excommunication business at all, Kevin. We're just increasing the distance between the parties.'

'The other crowd started the war, Pat. Come on now – they violated the majority will of the people.

Of course they shouldn't be allowed to remain within the folds of the Church.'

Pat holds up his hand. 'Leave it, Kevin, for now. I have a heavy day ahead of me.'

'If you need assistance …'

'No, I drew the lowest card. 'Tis down to me.'

'You did at that, but still, I'll help.'

'Not at all.' He thinks that it is best for the men to be with a priest who does not believe that they are getting their just desserts.

Afterwards, in his study, he looks at the names of the condemned men he had written on foolscap. He whispers each name.

What do I say to them? Is there a right thing to say? A wrong thing? Will words matter to them at all?

Should he be blunt, uncaring, matter of fact? Should he distance himself?

No. That is not possible for him. He is not of that kind. With growing dismay and frustration, he gets up and paces the study. He rights a painting of an eviction scene he had bought in a junk shop in Rush, runs a forefinger along a film of dust along a bookshelf. Her eyes are failing, he thinks, and still he refuses to wear spectacles. Sighs.

His hands are perspiring, shaky, and he has yet to meet any of the men.

It has not been bad so far; at least, not as bad as he had expected. He'd had a sense of dread about coming here and looking into the eyes of the men. Yes, he had looked into the eyes of the dying, of old men, of a child, even, but those eyes had belonged to the old and feeble, and it was no man's fault that they were being called to their eternal reward. This was different. On the battlefield, at least one has some chance, however slight, of surviving – but to bring men out and shoot them dead, in cold blood …

'Tis not fecking right, 'tis not fecking right.

The men have listened to what he had to say and most have been fine about it, resigned, though no doubt some are still in shock from the *other* news. Young O'Connor had shouted at him to get the fuck out of the cell and continued shouting until he reached a point where he broke down and began to cry.

Five down, two to go …

'This way, Father,' Tony the redcap says.

Stink of stale air, of urine stale and fresh, of boot polish, of paint and other smells he is unable to discern. The redcap leads the way up a winding iron staircase.

Father Pat looks up, through the glass roof. The skies are overcast, dark clouds moving quickly, like gossips hurrying bad news to each other.

Wanting to say something for the sake of it, he says, 'It's a cold one, Tony. The wind would carve you to the bone.'

'Deed it would, Fadder. There's no wind like a Curragh one for staling the heat out of you.'

In a whisper, outside the cell they've stopped at, he says, 'How's the poor unfortunate inside?'

'He refused breakfast. Something only those that want to stay healthy do in this scab of a place.'

Father Pat smiles at the man and his laconic delivery.

'The cooks in here would burn water, Father, honest to Christ.'

'No appetite, so. But then, bad news sours the stomach, isn't that so?'

'You're probably right.'

'It does.'

'Ah, well, I suppose, Father.'

'Given the circumstances, it's only to be expected.'

'Aye. By the way, the new Governor is worse than the other bollocks we had, and by Christ is that saying something.'

'Ah, now, Boyle had a bit of nature in him.'

'Why? Because you squeezed a dead corpse out of him?'

A dead corpse. Poor Behan …

The priest bites his lower lip to quell the spark of

a smile. 'It cost him his position – they moved him elsewhere. A big upheaval for his family, Tony.'

'Fuck him, Father – serves him right. He fined me three days for not shining the buttons on my great-coat. He's one thick man.'

'Ah, well …'

'Just bellow if you need us, Father. I heard one of the others giving you a hard time of it. As if their own foolishness was all your doing.'

'You couldn't blame him.'

Tony says, 'They've been quiet since they got word yesterday. Himself in the cell included – but then, he's the youngest of them and maybe because of that he's feeling it a bit more. I gave him beads. Try to be okay with him without it being too obvious, if you know what I mean?' He looks around to make his point – the walls have ears.

He turns a key in the door, pushes it open and walks in. 'Stand up, White, and show the padre a bit of respect.'

Oh Christ, he's so young. I doubt if he's even had his first shave.

Chalky lowers his feet to the floorboards and sits upright on the edge of the bunk, hands gripping a lump of mattress either side of him. Then he stands.

Tony says, 'Good man,' and turning to Father Pat, adds, 'I'll be outside if you need me, Father.'

He pulls the door behind him, leaving it ajar.

The silence in the cell is awkward. The young man resembles a boy Father Pat once knew very well.

There is the same apple-red freshness in the cheeks, the round eyes. Eddie Conway had died about three hours after falling from a pushbike, the handlebar catching his side, doing internal harm. Oh, got up fine and made light of the accident and then that night, riddled with pain in his stomach. He was fourteen. A death sentence of hours.

Aren't we all under a death sentence?

'Well, young White, how are you feeling?'

No answer.

The priest coughs. Awkward.

'You can sit on the edge of the bed if you want. No need for formalities here. Have you a cigarette? I came without my own – that Father Magee in the house, I swear to God but he lifts them every time I leave a packet out of my hand.'

'I've cigarettes, Father, but no matches.'

'Sure, Tony'll give us a match. What good is a red-cap only for carrying matches, eh?'

'He's not the worst of them – there's bastards worse than him in here.'

'I have to agree with you there. I know some of them.'

He steps outside onto the walkway, walks down to the redcap and says, 'Tony, would you strike up a light for us, like a good man?'

'Here's the box, Father. Hand them back on your way out. Can't have the boy burning his mattress – though it'd be hard for him to do that, it's wet from his pissing in it.'

'The nerves are at him – you'd be pissing on yourself too, Tony, would you not, if you knew that any morning now you'd be facing into a go of muzzles.'

'More than likely, Father, more than fucking likely.'

Back in the cell, he strikes a match, uses one hand to guard it from a draught and the other to bring it forward and down to the cigarette clasped between Chalky's lips. The flame casts a soft reddish-orange glow on the fresh face.

'You heard all the news, Father?'

'Yes, yes, I did. Bad news indeed.'

A pause – to signal there's more bad news to come.

Chalky says, 'We were expecting it, to be honest.'

'Bad news is always hard to take, even when we're expecting it.'

'No reprieve, either. Are they serious, Father? They're going to shoot us?'

Pause.

'Yes.'

'I hear the lads saying it's Collins's men who'll be doing the executing.'

'Collins is dead, so they're hardly his men any more.'

'They'll always be his men.'

'I suppose you're right.'

'At least they'll be good shots, won't they? They won't be nervous and go shooting us where they shouldn't. I'd hate to be shot in the stomach, cos that's the worse place to be shot.'

'So I hear – ah, I don't think that'll happen. Divil a fear of it.'

'Not with Collins's men anyway.'

'Not with Collins's men, I'm sure.'

'Being shot is better than being hung, Father.'

'Being shot is a soldier's death – the hanging is for cowards.'

'My poor mother, the little ones, they'll take it bad.'

'You're the eldest?'

'I am, Father. I would have been nineteen in January, a month to the very day that they're sending me west.'

Father Pat makes a noise like a breath is trapped in his throat.

He says, 'It's a good cigarette, this – I don't usually draw on a Woodbine. What's rare is lovely, they say. Deed I think that's a true saying.'

'Is that why we only die the once, Father?'

The touch of sarcasm, the edge of bitterness in it, surprises him. Though he is at a loss to see why this should be the case. Why wouldn't the lad be bitter and angry?

Chalky says, 'How're the other six bearing up?'

'Sure, don't you see them yourself?'

'I don't see them, I don't see us, the way you do, Father.'

'And what way is that?'

'Trapped men, waiting to be corpses.'

'Aren't we all that, son?'

'This is different, Father, don't you think?'

Father Pat sighs and then says, 'It is. I can't make sense of it at all.'

'Mangan thinks he's made sense of it – has he spoken to you?'

'Not yet. A grand footballer that lad, I hear.'

'He's some man to pluck a ball out of the air, Father. I was playing against him a while back – he jumped for this ball – I'm not codding you, the round tower was in the background on the hill – you know the tower, Father?'

He nods, thinks of a line from a bad poem, *for the Viking raider a tall eye was built in the Kildare sky* …

'Well, one moment the tower was in my full view and the next Mangan was soaring upwards, blotted out the tower he did. When he was landing he skulled me. Three stitches I'd to get.'

'I've heard good things about his skill, like I said.'

'No good to tip you a horse, Father. Thinks he knows racehorses, but he hasn't a clue. All he knows about horses is that they have a hoof at each corner.'

'Indeed. I must remember that – in case he gives me a tip.'

Chalky says quietly, 'There's no need for you to remember anything about us, Father.'

Father Pat says in a harsh whisper, 'Ah Christ, Chalky – why the bloody hell didn't youse hand in the weapons, take advantage of the amnesty and not be giving these boyos a chance to riddle youse?'

'The Cause, Father.'

'Cause my arse.'

'It's what I believe in, Father. What my father believed in and his before him.'

122

'And you believe in robbing shops, destroying the locomotives and railway lines and looting goods carriages and taking pot shots at Free State soldiers too, and look where it has you – your poor mother, you poor fool, you.'

Pause, a deep silence.

'We needed money to buy supplies – we didn't have a quartermaster we could run to and sign for what we needed. Not like those British lackeys out there. For instance, we bought the Lee Enfields from a soldier in Naas barracks and ammunition from another soldier. We …' Chalky shrugs, suddenly realising it doesn't matter what they bought and that what they had bought was the reason they were all in this unholy mess.

Father Pat draws on his cigarette and then exhales. 'What does Mangan know?' he says.

'Pardon, Father?'

'You said Mangan thinks he has made sense of things.'

'He'll probably tell you himself.'

'And what do you think of his sense?'

'He could be right.'

'Youse were found in a trench with weapons, ammunition, clothes – a proper little curiosity shop, I hear. You were all in violation of the amnesty. Of course you were aware of the consequences. What sense is there to make out of that?'

'The amnesty is an excuse to do away with us, Father. That's all it is – an excuse.'

'Do you really think so, Chalky?'

Abrupt creak of floorboards as Chalky stands up. Father Pat inhales a deep breath. Waits. One can never be sure what a condemned man is capable of doing – an unhinged mind cares for nothing.

'Steady, Father, just moving to the window. I like to catch the sun in my face. There's a small bird sings in the mornings. I don't know what kind – he does land on a ledge somewhere above me and sings his little heart out, and when it stops singing, I know it's time.'

'Time for what, Chalky?'

'For another day to begin – when you see the end of your days in sight, Father, when you … your memories become clearer. Nature's touches, your mother's smile, the feel of grass on your bare feet. You're amazed at how clearly you can see and smell these memories.'

A sharpening of the senses – the last uses of them.

'I'll be praying for you and the others, Chalky.'

'What else would a priest do, Father?'

In other words, *What use is he?*

'You'll be wanting to write a letter or letters – the others are. I'll give them to your mother.'

The air turns cold. Father Pat sees the change in the young man's face, as if another part of his world had just collapsed in on him.

'Are we not being allowed visitors?'

'I'm sorry, Chalky – they sent me round to break the news.'

'It's that bastard Kearney, the snaky officer, isn't it?

He made the decision?'

'That information wasn't divulged to me, but I suspect there's an element of truth in what you say. But it is also a general policy, Chalky.'

'It would've been nice to say a proper goodbye.'

'I doubt if there's any such thing.'

'Are we your first?'

'First?'

'To see being executed?'

'Yes.'

Chalky leans his back against the wall under the window. A curious halo of light rests above his head, an arc of brightness, and then cloud shadow banishes it.

'They don't want word getting out about what really happened.'

'I can't bring myself to conjecture, lad – my mind has enough on its plate.'

The confessional, the soldier, the killing of Behan... Conjecture? You don't have to conjecture.

'I was never good at writing, Father. Would you write down what I have to say?'

'Wouldn't that be a privilege for me?'

'It would.'

Father Pat smiles. Moore was the same, made dry quips.

'They killed Behan, our commandant, at Moore's Bridge, Father. He was shot in the shoulder and then by the side of the truck because he was kicking up a racket. We all were – they shot him and the shock of it quietened us.'

'They say he was shot while trying to escape through a window in the holding cell where youse were being held. That he wouldn't desist …'

They say. But I know the truth.

'How it happened, Father, is how I've told you.'

The priest remains silent.

'Father?'

'What, Chalky?'

'Where's Dooley?'

'Dooley?'

'He was in the dug-out with us.'

'I don't know where he is.'

'And Eddie Hennigan?'

'He was caught outside the dug-out, and he's only sixteen. He's out. I heard it spoke of last night.'

Officers slapping themselves on the back for their display of clemency.

He thinks, *Generally they tell me little and what little I'm told I've already figured out for myself. Except in a few instances, this being one of them: Where's Dooley?*

'Does it not interest you, make you suspicious, Father, why those two aren't with us?'

'If they're not here, they don't interest me – why should they? The woman and her daughters – one would have to be suspicious of them, too.'

'Not Nora, no – not her.'

'And that is Mangan's sense of it all? Why the gang of you are to be executed? Sure, boy, if they wanted no one to find out about what happened to Behan, they'd have silenced the informers too. Yes?'

'They wouldn't shoot them. If they started that they'd soon be turning their guns on their own soldiers, too – the ones who bet us in and out of the ground the night they found us.'

'If they were informers, Chalky, didn't they put themselves in harm's way by being caught in the farmhouse with youse?'

'That's a thought I didn't think of, Father. But the fact is, they're not here.'

'Yes, well, you're right, they're not.'

'And we aren't a gang, Father – we're part of the 6th Battalion Column.'

Consider yourself reprimanded, Father.

'I meant no offence.'

'Did you not?'

'No.'

Silence, interrupted by indistinct voices on the landing, patchy sentences. Words like: *The medical orderly … The CO said … When are you off duty?*

Tony soft-spoken, the other gruff.

Father Pat says, 'It's said that 'twas the searchlight on the roof of the Water Tower found youse out. Great bars of light sweep across the land, and …'

'I know about the searchlight. All about it, Father. They're saying that so the informer will be able to walk around the town in safety after we're gone.'

'Perhaps you're right.'

'After we're gone, who'll dare to touch him? No one. We're to be a lesson, Father. A warning.'

'A sad lesson. A brutal warning.'

'I won't be allowed to put any of that in my letter, will I?'

'No – they'll scribble over the parts they want omitted. If needs be, the orderly room clerk will write the letter anew and give it back to me. You'll not be afforded much scope beyond saying your goodbyes, I'm afraid.'

Chalky's face pinches tight under the blow of an idea, an unspoken request.

'What is it, Chalky?'

'You could sneak a letter out for me.'

'Why? So you could breathe revenge into the hearts of your brothers? No, the sooner this business of bloodletting stops, the better for us all. Your commandant has already asked this of me.'

The silence seems to say, *Fair enough.*

'Three days, Father.'

'The nineteenth. It's marked on my calendar – I'm going to detest that date for the rest of my days.'

'Six days before Christmas.'

Ah now, son …

'Hard heads and harder hearts, Chalky – they're not for turning. Don't live the rest of your hours on that hope.'

'Remember what I said to you, Father – the reason we were done for.'

As if I didn't already know.

'Isn't it hard to make sense of things, Father?'

'Sense of things? Only the man above can do that.'

Chalky, my son, Father Pat wants to say, *forget about revenge, about who did what to put you in here. The kernel of the matter is this – you are here because of you.*

He doesn't say this because he knows that in the days left to him, Chalky will realise that for himself.

The prison's sergeant-major in his office, a stout and balding figure with a nose carrying a reddish bump, a legacy of a bad break and a worse setting, talks hoarsely about the coming days. How events will unfold, the operation order and the chaplain's role. The man has no empathy for the condemned men, his tone only revealing concern that 'everything goes okay'.

Without a hitch.

He cannot stand to hear the man speak as though the executions were some inconvenient spur-of-the-moment drill parade foisted upon him by some daft commanding officer, and excuses himself with an abruptness that causes the NCO to stare at him from under wild eyebrows.

'Don't let me keep you, Father.'

He crosses the yard to the blue wooden door close to the MP hut. The wind pushes against steel double doors used to access vehicular traffic in and out of the Glasshouse. The yard here has a floor of loose stones. The door is bolted and locked. He waits for the redcap to finish speaking with a civilian employee, to leave his hut and see him out.

What a desolate place this is, he thinks. The sun must

think twice about shining in here, that it's a waste of time trying to charm bad air.

By a flowerbed, in a wheelbarrow partially covered by a sheet of hessian sacking, rests a thick wooden stake, a bag of cement, a shovel, a spade, a pickaxe and strands of thick tug-of-war rope.

He feels the surfacing of wounds from his youth; burned palms, blisters full of fluid he'd pierced that night with the tip of a red-hot sewing needle.

Ah, I was good at the tug-of-war, powerful. For a few moments he is in a field on a summer's day, the hay in, the sun yellowing the grass, the annual field day – the community get-together, athletic contests and chasing the greasy pig. The fiddle and beat of the bodhrán, blisters cooled by beer bottles that had been left to chill in the river's edge.

'Father, that stuff in the barrow – they're getting ready for the boys,' the redcap says in a low voice, as though he were divulging a secret, as though the priest had not the insightfulness to suss for himself the whys of the wheelbarrow's contents.

Outside the Glasshouse, he composes his thoughts. Breathes in deeply and holds the breath, exhales. Aye, there is a difference between free air and prison air.

He breathes again, exhales.

He looks down the sweep of road to Hare Park Internment Camp, the rows of tar-felt roofs, the creosoted wooden huts, and then directly across at Sandes Soldiers' Home. He'd met Elizabeth Sandes only the once, a pleasant and remarkable woman who through her determination had set up places where soldiers could relax, read, enjoy billiards, coax them away from engaging in vice in the nearby towns by offering them an alternative lifestyle. Nineteen homes all over the Empire, wherever a British soldier stood watch – at least the Irish officers had the good sense to allow her home to remain open. That some of them can actually stop short of doing things to spite themselves and their own. Venerable and old, she'd retired north, to Antrim, he had heard. To die on familiar ground – dare he think it – to die on land where the shadow of the Union Jack still flies.

He feels within his bones a strange sort of disfranchisement, as though something is missing within him that he once owned, was sure was his, and now isn't sure at all.

'Tis called faith, *Father.*

I believe. I believe.

Yes, your faith is rock solid.

Yes.

He is about to set off when a staff car pulls up in front of the gates. The new Governor, no doubt, Tony's friend – will he detest the sight of dull buttons?

No. Kearney.

There's a thing: you're nearly always guaranteed to meet the wrong people at the most inappropriate time, when you're feeling as low as an ancient and long-fallen tombstone.

'Father,' Kearney says, pulling on his tunic cuffs in turn, like he is wearing something on his wrists he doesn't want anyone to see, a dead man's watch or cards he has yet to play.

'Art.'

The saying of his name, attaching no greeting to it, says enough, the priest thinks.

'The car is going back up the camp – do you want a lift?'

Father Pat shakes his head. 'I need both the air and the exercise.'

Kearney signals for the driver to drive on and moves to the prison door.

The smell of diesel hangs in the air. Pat wonders if mankind has traded ass and horse dung on the roads for a more invisible sort of dung? Fumes from exhaust? No doubt. There was always shite in the world and there'll always be shite in the world of one sort or another.

Aren't you the man full of diverse thoughts? Be in the now, Father.

He is a dapper little man, the priest thinks, in his starched uniform and brown webbing. Groomed moustache, clean hands, no dirt under the fingernails, glossy brown shoes. You wouldn't think at first glance that he had a vicious streak. It's the way his eyes hold yours that alert you – they have an icy grip. Clean hands, which is not to say there is no dirt on them.

Kearney puts his hand on the knocker. 'Father, would you take a look at this?' The knocker is heavily bound in a white rag, tied with twine. He raps on the door with his knuckles, and calls, 'Corporal.'

Turning to look at Pat, he says, 'Well, Father, you've done your duty for the day?'

There's a well-buried barb for you. *You do your duty and I'll do mine.*

'I have.'

'So we won't see you now till the morning of the executions …'

'I'll be here the evening before, to say Mass, hear confessions and collect their letters and if they want to see me before then, they've only to ask and a visit will be granted, isn't that so?'

'If the acting governor approves.'

'I'm sure he will.'

'I'm not actually sure if *I* will.'

The priest tries to disguise his dismay. The officer turns from him, raps on the door again.

'So, judge, jury and executioner,' Father Pat says.

'Not judge, no. Jury and executioner – I can live with that.'

A metal plate head high in the door slides back. Father Pat sees the redcap's eyes in the rectangle of space.

'Sir.'

'Open up, and be a bit bloody smartish about it.'

He turns square on to Father Pat. 'You shouldn't become too personal with the men – you'll end up taking their deaths too personally, as if they were close friends or family even.'

'Personal? No. But the way this whole business is being conducted is unsavoury and invites serious questioning.'

'Good. You might question the bastard who shot my brother – who walked over and put a revolver in his mouth and blew his brains all over the fucking road, Father.'

The door opens. The officer readdresses his focus.

'Corporal, what the fuck is that doing ragged up?'

'The wind bangs it, Sir. Sure, I do be checking out every five seconds to find no one there.'

'Ghosts, eh?' Kearney says.

Perhaps, Father Pat thinks, angels coming in to comfort *the lost.*

Oh, and you've seen ghosts and angels, have you?

No.

The priest says, 'Those men in there didn't kill your brother.'

'They're on the same side, Father,' Kearney says, keeping his back to the priest, staring straight ahead through the full of the open door.

'Sir,' the redcap says, saluting.

Not showing the flat of the hand as the British do, but its side. We do things differently to prove to ourselves that we're different from them. Ah, the centuries – the scribes say the Normans became as Irish as the Irish themselves. But during the hundreds of years that we had been theirs, we had become as English as the English. Certainly, their capacity for acts of callousness is now inherent in us. 'Revenge, Captain—'

The door closes hard, the muffled knocker a silent action.

In the study he shares with Father Kevin, he sits in an easy chair staring out the bay window at the night, the stars, the eyelash of moon. His tea on the sill has gone cold, cheese sandwiches remain untouched.

He sits in the dark, only a solitary candle lit on the mantelpiece. In a moment now, the searchlight will be powered on and the great beam will throw great swathes of light on the camp's approach roads and the plains for miles around.

An informer? Most likely.

Dooley – the talk, if not the evidence, points to him. No doubt had his own agenda: money; to ensure his survival; to get out of the mess he was in. Who knows? Only Dooley.

The country is full of informers. Judas Land. Our history is awash with their input. People tell tales on each other all the time and secrets – Jasus – too hot for their tongues to hold. The full truth of the circumstances will never be found out. Already he can see what's at play. Coffin earth thrown on the truth. Behan's death ... rumours and counter-rumours, the witnesses to it soon to be silenced, the ordinary soldier will restrict himself to speaking of it in the confessional or amongst themselves, shutting up whenever someone who wasn't there that night enters their company. The truth of it all will be lost in the graininess of time, as each witness takes his leave to the grave - the silence of the heart, the silence of tongues. There are times when people won't talk, and such a time is when a terrible injustice will have been done.

From the eyes of the future, the bones of the truth? Those living in the decades ahead will say …

Men died and they died in awful ways during terrible times. It's time to move on. And so many atrocities – where does one begin to search for the truth? And if the truth be found, what of it? This far on, it changes nothing. War – a glorious death?

Will they say that of this generation? We saw glory in war – honourable deaths? Or will they think that eighteen was too young to die, to be brought from a cell and shot dead when the morning wasn't yet full of itself? God knows what they will think of us, what they will blame on us.

He is pulled from deep thought by Kevin's sudden and unexpected arrival. He tugs a cord and the electric light blinks and hisses.

'Oh, you're up! And sitting in the dark, Pat.'

'Yes, trying to throw some light on matters.'

'Ah, God, haven't you the dry wit.' Kevin's cheeks are flushed – tippling in the officers' mess again. He goes to the cabinet, lowers the drop-leaf and pours brandy into short glasses, sighing and blowing as if the effort of pouring was a huge physical strain.

'A nightcap – you'll join me? Ah, you will, of course.'

'I will.'

Father Kevin falls wearily into the opposite chair. Lounges in it, grey hairs on the back of his long fingers, nicotine-stained forefinger, dark brown like he'd an accident at his toiletry – his own as bad. They sip at their brandies.

'You were talking to Kearney this morning?' Father Kevin says.

'I was.'

'A grand chap.'

Father Pat does not disagree. Nothing he could possibly say would alter Kevin's estimation of the man.

'I have something to ask of you,' Father Kevin says, straightening himself, uncrossing those spidery legs and sitting to the edge of his seat, leaning forward. 'Though perhaps it is too late at night to speak of the matter.'

'What is it?'

'They'd prefer if I took over ministering to the lads.'

Pat boils over inside, but stays his tongue and then says, 'Who would prefer?'

'The general staff.'

'I see.' He waits for a few seconds to see whether Kevin will volunteer a reason for the request. 'Why?' he asks, his voice short of hard.

'They think I have more experience.'

'They think you're one of them, you mean.'

'Now, Pat, let's not.'

'Yes, let's do – you're in their company every night, playing cards, drinking with them – more friend than pastor to them. I don't see you down drinking with the men in their canteens and messes. Are you out of bounds there?'

The hand with the grey hairs goes up and down in

placatory waves, like a seagull hovering above the sea in wait of prey.

'Pat, we have the rank of captain – why would I drink with the men? Do you think they'd relax with a priest, an officer, albeit their spiritual officer, in their midst?'

'Next you'll be telling me that you're going to hear only the confessions of officers.'

'I was asked to ask you.'

'You have asked. I'll look after the men.'

'I was asked to ask you and then I was told to tell you that it is me who'll be doing the taking care of the men.'

'I hope you told them differently.'

Kevin sighs long and hard, sits back in the chair, crosses his legs, perches his chin on his hand. 'Yes, I told them differently. I said it would be cruel on the men to take you from them now, at this late stage – they know you.'

Father Pat nods. 'Thank you.'

'I didn't tell them that I also think it's cruel on you to be with them.'

'It's not.'

'I'm afraid it is, Pat. You think too much, you question the ins and outs of everything. You wonder what people a hundred years from now will think of us. You analyse matters to death – beyond death, even. We've spoken together many times on this and like subjects.'

'Isn't that what we should do? Ask the questions, find the answers?'

'Not about some things. You learn to accept, Pat – you need to learn to accept.'

'Accept? As in accept what?'

'That death comes to us all in various guises. You must have faith, absolute faith in God that even if we don't know what He's at, He does. That's faith – pure acceptance.'

The men sip at their brandies.

Father Kevin says, 'Not a good vintage, this, is it?'

'No.'

'Accept, Pat, have faith. Do you ever stop to ask yourself what the people who lived a hundred years ago thought of us?'

'No.'

'Why not? Does it not matter to you what their thoughts were?'

'You have me there, I'm afraid. It's something I—'

'If you had faith, you'd know without doubt that there is a life after death.'

What he is telling you is this – be more of a priest and less of a philosopher.

'So what? We give up on the living, surrender meekly to the injustice and the suffering?'

'No, we don't – you fight the good fight and accept without bitterness or exultation the results of our endeavours. We have a job to do – we shake hands with the devil – and there's a devil in all of us. A devil in the adverse circumstances in which we find ourselves. You have to trust in Him.'

To deliver us from evil …

Their last full day of life is almost complete. Father Pat had anticipated an air of impenetrable doom and was surprised at the almost surreal gaiety, the easy conversation, smiles and laughter, and suspicious of it too. He wondered if it was a front and reached the conclusion that though the prevailing atmosphere was part charade, there also existed a lightness that could not be anything less than genuine. Perhaps it was sheer joy that the waiting, this part of their suffering, was almost done with, that at the very least the worst that could happen to them would soon be over?

By this time tomorrow, the rounds in the Lee Enfields will be spent, casings lying about the feet of the firing party all gathered, the remains of the executed dressed in brown habits and fitted into pine coffins, earth lying fresh on a mass grave in the Glasshouse yard, a little corner near a boundary wall. The families will know and the officers will drink their fill in their comfortable mess and the politicians in Dublin smug and content in the knowledge that they'd demonstrated a ruthlessness to their adversaries, sufficient enough to indicate their resolve to win the war at all costs, to succeed where the British had failed: to break the spine of a guerrilla organisation.

He folds his stole and puts it and the silver chalice into his black leather bag, all three a parting present from his parishioners in Dundrum. He hands the empty wine bottle to a redcap. He'd passed the chalice round to the condemned men – each sipped and had partaken of the Host. A sip of wine to ease the way. Medicine of Christ. The Bread of Life. What of the firing party? Will those men sleep easily tomorrow night? Yes – they're soldiers and had obeyed orders and after all they had killed men who had been intent on killing them, and but for the grace of God had not.

The condemned have retired to their cells for supper. He had heard all their confessions, sins too ordinary and hardly sins at all, nothing irreparable nor unforgivable. The residue of their actions and non-actions troubled them greatly now that they were acutely aware there was neither time nor opportunity left for them to make amends: a theft of money from a mother's purse, impure thoughts about a woman, a loss of temper with a child, an unmentionable thing said in the heat of temper that drove a distance that was never reduced between father and son, the edge of a broken bottle put to a man's face, an act of intercourse with a married woman, the touching of the private area for sexual gratification … human things.

Flaws.

Tony, the friendly redcap with the unfriendly face, is on night duty and had stood at the back of the small hall throughout Mass.

Father Pat says, 'Ah, Tony …'

'There's tae after being made, Father.'

'I'll say goodnight to the men and collect their letters, and then I'll go with you.'

'That's no problem. Samuels is duty officer tonight and he's not a difficult man. The other bastard could show up at any time – he's like that, you know, doesn't like to give a body peace of mind. If it had ears to listen, he'd bother his own arsehole with his tongue.'

'Now, Tony.'

'Sorry, Father.'

A call from a redcap leaning over the railing on the second floor: 'The lads want to know are you collecting the letters, Father?'

'I'm on my way.'

'You know I have to take them from you, Father. You'll get them back in the morning, after you know yourself.'

'I understand, Tony.'

'Weren't they in right good form, considering?'

'Yes – remarkably good cheer, considering.'

Their demeanour was in no way bitter or resentful. They seemed almost perfectly happy to be going, boisterous, slagging each other, shaking each other's hands. Moore had called them together at the end of Mass and told them to go out and die like the soldiers they were, that he was proud to be dying in their company, to have fought with them. Head up, remember.

He leaves Chalky until last. This part of the night had lasted longer than he had thought it would. A couple of the men had broken down in the privacy of their cells and these he had cajoled and patched up as best he could. But the night was theirs to contend with. He pitied them their cross. Another who insisted he wanted to leave no letter to his next of kin changed his mind and he had to pen a few lines for him because his hands had the tremors.

He pushes in the cell door. No sense in knocking because the lad is expecting a visit.

'Stay sitting. Don't get up on my account, son.'

'That was a nice Mass, Father. They were nice things you said about us.'

'Thank you, Chalky. Sure, you *are* brave men. You're all going straight to Heaven, every last jack of you.' He adds, drawing his hand from his pocket, 'I brought the cigarettes this evening. And the matches.'

They smoke. Chalky is shivering, his breaths of smoke coming out in hurried little puffs.

He says, teeth chattering, 'I heard the lorry coming in this evening. It was them?'

'It was – Collins's men.'

'Laughing and joking like they were heading off to work on the bogs.'

'Men do that, Chalky. They're hiding their nerves.'

'They went off then to have a few pints, lucky yokes.'

'Yes.'

'Not too many, I hope – the drink could give them the jitters. We wouldn't want that.'

'They'll consume just enough to steady their nerves.'

'I want to see their faces – I don't want to be blind-folded.'

'It'll be as you wish, son, but if it were me, I'd go for the blindfold. I'd wear ten of them.'

'Closing your eyes would be the same thing.'

'I suppose.'

'What happens, Father?'

He ponders the question for several seconds and then says, 'When you die?'

'No, in the morning. The truth now, Father.'

Truth? He wants truth.

'You'll be led out, son, into the yard, tied to a pole close to the wall. The officer will ask you if want a last smoke, offer the blindfold, and then he'll march to the side of the firing party and give the order.'

Silence between the men. Laughter beyond the prison cell, redcaps.

'Do you think they're right to be doing what they're doing to us, Father? Do we deserve this? Does my mother?'

'You know my thoughts – it isn't right.'

'Thos had the right idea – we should have gone down fighting.'

'It'll be quick. It beats an old man's death in a hospital.'

'They should have allowed us visitors. It was mean of them not to.'

'I did ask. I went to the mess for tea and in the evening for a jar and spoke to the camp OC and other officers that I thought might have his ear, but sure, I may as well have stuck out my tongue and wagged it at the stars for all the bloody good it did me.'

'At least you tried.'

'Hand on my heart, I tried my living best.'

Had gone so far to make a call to Cosgrave himself, the President, but was not put through. Not available, he was told.

'I knew you would, Father.'

'Your letters …'

'I've kept them short.'

'I thought I was to write them for you?'

'Ah no, Father, I was grand by myself. Thanks anyhow.'

'Fine, so. 'Tis better in your own words.'

Indeed, he feels a little relieved that he did not have to write the lad's last words, for reading the others and writing the one had put a strain in him.

Chalky reaches under his pillow and removes his three letters and hands them to the priest.

'I'll make sure your mother gets these.'

'Thanks, Father.'

They smoke for a few moments, the priest thinking he ought to be going, the youth thinking it was time for him to be alone.

'You'll be here in the morning, Father? At what time?'

'First thing – about half past six.'

'Wasn't it good of Moore, Father?'

'Yes. By God that was an officerly thing to do, to swap the number he'd drawn.'

'I didn't mind being last to go west, Father.'

'He knew that, but he wanted to see his men off first. And between us, Chalky, it's good that you're going first. It'll be hard play on the nerves of the others as they listen to the shots ring out. Hard play indeed.'

'One by one, Father. In twos would have been quicker.'

'Errah, you know what armies are like. Worse than the Church for having their rituals.'

'I suppose so.'

'The waiting is a torture in itself. It's good that you'll be going first – you have someone's prayers …'

A loose smile broke on Chalky's face. 'If I had, Father, I wouldn't be here in the first place.'

'Haven't we to be grateful for small mercies? The smallest of them even.'

'When it's over …'

'I'll be right over to you, lad, giving you a blessing, the last rites.'

How many acts of the last rite do you intend giving these men?

'They'll give us back then.'

The priest is puzzled for a moment, then understands.

'Yes,' he says, but there is something in him that gives off an uncertainty that Chalky is quick to pick up on.

'Our remains, to our families.'

Christ, the trouble I had getting Behan back to his family

— they moved on the Governor, a nice man, punished for doing a Christian thing.

'For waking and the like – for the family's goodbye to me? Don't say they are if they're not, Father.'

You do know. There is trouble in the young man's heart. Look at the added hurt in his face.

'I'll make sure it happens.'

How will you make sure? You, who has Kearney's ear …

Kevin will assist.

Chalky says, 'If it doesn't happen, Father, it'll be another hard cross I'll have put on my mother's back.'

'Leave it to me. Don't you worry yourself on that score.'

'I dreamt last night about the lads – they blew a hole in the wall and freed us. It felt as though it was really happening. Then I woke and the first thing I noticed was the silence.'

'The silence.'

'The bird – I saw it this morning. Maybe it's not the song bird, but just a glimpse of a redbreast,' Chalky says, looking out at a night that hasn't a star to call its own.

Chalky

There is, Chalky thinks, a lot to be said for death catching you by surprise. It's over before you are aware – Thos, for instance. While he must have thought death was always a possibility because of the game he was in, he didn't know that on that particular evening of evenings he would be cornered like a rat and all would end for him on the plains, his blood spilling on the grass, onto sheep dirt and scrawny thistle beds.

It was over for him before he had much of a chance to realise that it was.

On the other hand, if one is aware he is going to die, it leaves him time to prepare, to put his affairs in order, to say goodbye. In the normal course of events, then, it's better to have some notice of your demise – however, these are not normal times. He had received notice, yet was afforded no opportunity to put his affairs in order or to say his goodbyes, to leave a lasting goodbye in someone's memory and not through the written word, which when you think on it is no proper way to say goodbye.

It is pitch black and biting cold in his cell. He had said his prayers, a decade of Hail Marys and another of Our Fathers.

His mind is racing, thoughts whirring along like flotsam in a quick-flowing river. He sees things more clearly than he had ever done now that there's not much need for him to see things so clearly.

This morning, he shaved. He shaves once a week; it's all he has need of, for the growth in him is thin and poor, like arse whiskers on an oul' lad, Johnston had said, not liking it at all when Chalky said, 'How come you're familiar with oul' lads' arses?'

All over, bar the shouting. Bar the final prayers, the flurry of lead, the shroud and the coffin, the heavy kisses of earth, the final pats of shovel on the grave.

He tries to still his thoughts by fixing an image of his mother in his head. At this time of night, she has probably finished saying her prayers and is having a cup of tea. She is an awful woman for tea. Sheila might be with her, or Wilson. Seanie and Anto might be up too, wanting tea, hoping Wilson had brought with him a half pound of biscuits from Nolan's General Merchants. Wilson is good at doing things like that, bringing little treats. *What night is it? Monday. How could I forget? Monday. Wilson …*

Mondays he has a few pints in Harte's Hotel on the square and listens to the wireless old man Harte bought but is too deaf to hear. He won't visit because Mam does not like the smell of drink in the house. Hadn't she argued with Chalky about it?

'You're like your father,' she'd said, making it clear that this comparison was nothing to be proud of.

'There was little sunshine about my Sonny,' she sometimes said.

So, she is alone, sitting by the fire, letting the heat nurse her bad veins. She'll stare deep into the fire as he had often seen her do, and perhaps then she'll lift her thoughts from the fire and fix them on the positive aspects of her life, Anto and Seanie and how she at least still has them. A book might fall on the bedroom floor, a definite thud, disturbing her thoughts, or one of the lads cry out for her …

Do the lads miss him? He misses them, the craic he got out of each, rising them. Anto losing his head and saying he'd beat him into seven shades of shite and he with not a muscle in his arm. Seanie, the quiet one who didn't like being teased, and exacted revenge days, perhaps a week, afterwards by letting the air down in Chalky's tyres or giving him a false message to say Thos wanted him in the field at nine.

She won't miss washing out my sheets.

No more of that, no more hiding that from anyone – a kidney thing, she said. Maybe so.

Fearful, anxious, grounded a little by the companionship of his cigarettes and a pint – yes, maybe a kidney thing, but also a nerve thing. He had his grandfather's weak bladder and poor kidneys and his Aunt Eileen's scraggy nerves.

Moore saw the nerves.

Head up. Go like a soldier.

Like a soldier. Don't be shitting yourself. They say it happens involuntarily, the release.

Mangan said he was going to put his mind elsewhere, on the pitch, at the races.

Where will I put myself? At my mother's hearth? Or a place with someone?

Alice …

He had let his mother down. And Alice. She was his guardian angel and he did not know. If he'd listened to her, gone round at the time she'd asked, he wouldn't be here now. He might very well regret not being here and perhaps the lads inside might think him the informer, but regret or blame or whatever, he would still, after tomorrow morning, be breathing and have Alice, be on good terms with his mother and own his life and all the good and all the bad that came with it.

A dirty war.

A nation shitting on itself.

Pitch black. *Think of what you could have done differently.*

He leaves his mother behind at the gate and goes up by the church, but instead of going to the Railway Arms Hotel, he doubles back, intent on going to see Alice. Mangan and Johnston will wait a few minutes for him in the alley and then go on their way – they wouldn't dare call to his mother's, as she'd run them from the door before. They wouldn't know where to look for him. Alice …

Funny, isn't it, to be lying on his bunk in the dark, alone for his last hours, not thinking so much of the life he had led, but more of the one he has no chance of living.

All his sins and the harm he'd done are behind him.

It's not going to be in him to harm or help anyone. Isn't that what they mean by a holy soul? An entity who, through his death, no longer has the capacity to commit sin?

The silence of the Glasshouse.

Not a noise – the beating heart is silent. O'Connor, he was sure, had cried out, but after that, nothing – the silent noise of waiting, the walls, the beating hearts aware of what the morning will bring. And so the air is taut with apprehension and awkwardness and a feeling that by merely being held captive with condemned men, prisoner and redcap, they are about to be somehow tainted for the rest of their lives by this remote association.

God, do a miracle for me. Open up holes in these walls so the boys and me can escape – it's a little enough miracle to ask for, isn't it? I'm not testing you, for I believe in you with all my heart. I'm not going to be bitter like O'Connor, who told the priest that praying to you was like wasting breath on dead embers.

He is tired, too tired to sleep. There are moments when his heart thumps wildly and his stomach is sick.

He touches himself as he thinks of Alice. Naked in her sister's house, he sandwiched between her slim legs, the touch of her nipples against his flesh. He comes, softly groaning into his pillow that is for a moment his lover's bare shoulder.

Calming himself, fixing his clothes, wiping his hands in the towel in which he had caught his seed, he closes his eyes. Sinner, sinner.

He forgives, the priest's voice says.

Unlike others.

Whispers his prayers, again and again, concentrating on the words, turning the rosary beads Tony gave him, shutting out the world, lapsing every so often but only for milliseconds on faces he can't blot out: Mam's, Anto's, Seanie's and that of his father. Alice. Then he is away again, numbing his pain with prayer. Because, he thinks, at the end of the day, he knows no other way of escape.

Mam will cope, she is strong.

It is not yet bright when the Glasshouse awakens. The groans of a tyrannical soul yawning, stretching, barking up phlegm, feet on the march, redcaps tapping on the doors with their batons. Sixty-odd souls summoned from their night tombs, the hard souls, the ones who need to be taught more of a lesson than the internees in Hare Park – the tough nuts, the ones who brought the baton and other tortures on themselves, who change idealisms by small degrees till finally they decide they had given too much blood, sweat and tears to what had become a futile cause.

The rebels had brought their rebels to heel.

Does he want to eat breakfast? No.

Tea? No, it would run through me.

A cigarette? Certainly.

A swig of brandy – for the nerves? A swig, then.

The quietest silence of the night falls on the Glasshouse. He hears the firing party march along the stones in the yard, stop, turn in, stand easy. After breakfast they had moved him from an upstairs cell to a downstairs one, nearest the exit door behind the iron security railing that faces the lower floor. All the prisoners had been returned to their cells and locked up to prevent a riot. A few had shouted *God bless* and one said, 'You're martyrs, the lot of ye, we won't forget – by Christ, we won't ever forget!'

Mangan shouts – you can depend on Mangan to say something funny – 'So you're giving up the cigarettes and the whiskey, boy? Good for you.'

The priest enters his cell. He has on a white surplice and a purple stole, carries a Bible in one hand and a phial of holy water in the other.

Solemnly he makes the sign of the cross and sprinkles the water, 'Chalky, it's time.'

It is.

His knees are watery and he is tearful, hands shaking. So many thoughts in his head. He steps outside the cell behind a redcap and in front of another. The priest leads the way. The priest's name? Can't remember. *Father … you thundering eejit.* Brother Pius, wielder of the stick across knuckles. Skinner Pius, dead now.

God be good to him.

You don't mean that? Mangan's voice.

No.

The priest reads from the Bible as the tiny group walks out into the exercise yard, across to a door in the inner wall – a short walk, and yet it feels like miles. The morning is bright, the air clear and the skies blue but fringed with dark clouds to the west. Beyond this doorway, he stops abruptly at the sight of the six firers. Dressed in best uniform, all owning a moustache, none of them young, none skinny. Big, bulky men, a couple with red apple cheeks and eyes that look straight and seem not to notice his arrival.

The officer comes to him. His face is familiar from the night at Moore's Bridge and the visit to his cell – Buckley. There is no compassion in his grey eyes, his nod is as strong as a push and the procession lurches forward again.

They bind him, chest and ankles, to the post with thick, sinewy rope. Hangman's rope. Thick twine smell. Fix a white rectangular patch across the line of his chest, his heart the target. He is trembling. His breath haws the air, comes in little puffs of cloud. He wets himself, a slow release, a dribble. He breathes in air, holds it, releases. Such a simple …

'Blindfold?' Buckley asks neutrally.

He nods.

And it is fitted.

Feet disturbing the stones is the noise of Buckley taking his place at the side of the party, the priest saying the prayers, 'Hail Mary …'

Pause.

On Buckley's command, rifles cocked, one later than the others.

His breath comes hard.

'Take aim … fire!'

A volley of shots – dead before the report reaches his ears.

Silence.

Father Pat

''Tis a dirty job you had,' Father Kevin says in the kitchen, minutes after they had both sat to the table, an hour in from their varying affairs of the day.

'Yes, dirty,' Father Pat says quietly, peeling an apple. 'Filthy dirty.'

'And yet noble when you think on it. You held the souls of those men in your hands. You helped release them. You gave them hope and belief in the hereafter.'

'I gave them nothing.'

'Solace is worthy of note and you gave them that.'

'Did I?' *I saw neither solace nor acceptance in their features, only dread. Terror.*

Earlier, Mrs Caulfield the housekeeper had drawn the deep pleated curtains against the night. She had stayed on till six to learn some details of the day's events, but found both men unwilling to discuss the matter, at least in her presence. Having sussed that neither was in the humour for talking, she left quite soon after their arrival. She would hear all the news from Polly in MacDonagh officers' mess. What Polly didn't know wasn't worth knowing.

The potbelly stove throbs with heat. Flakes of turf sparkle and die on the lid, like stars burning to oblivion, souls extinguished. The older priest rolls up his shirtsleeves, revealing slender, freckly forearms that are filmed with fairish hair.

'I'm melting,' he says, spooning a clove from his hot whiskey onto a side plate.

His nose is red, full of the winter cold. He sniffles and blows into a handkerchief. There is, he can't fail but notice, not so much as a *God bless you* from Pat, and he is usually so full of manners and politeness. Bred in him to refrain from engaging in confrontation, but sometimes goes against the grain to his detriment.

'Look, Pat, it's over.'

'It'll never be over – never. How can it be?'

'You did all you could.'

'Which wasn't very much.'

'Which was all you could do in the set of circumstances allotted to you.'

Father Pat, tears in his eyes and a slight shake in his hands, says, 'And this holding onto the …'

'They'll get them back, eventually.'

'You asked?'

'There's no point. Give me a day or so.'

'That bastard Kearney. It's his doing, isn't it?'

'Not just his, I would safely venture.'

'He's—'

'Whist, will you? He's a lad you want little doings with – take that advice. Nasty work, he is, dealing with nasty types.'

So, keep away from Kearney, Father Pat thinks. *If Kevin can't reason with him, then what hope have I – someone for whom he has scant regard?*

'Pat, people will be looking to you for comfort and advice, but more than that, they'll be looking at you and do you know what it is they're expecting to see?'

No answer.

'Do you?'

'Yes – strength, a rock of faith … a rock.'

'Well then, be a fucking rock for them and not a bloody pile of sand.'

He had never heard the older priest breathe a swear word before and now understands the older man's depth of disappointment and exasperation with him. He reaches over and puts the apple peel in the stove and the apple with it, lets the lid slam shut.

What else does he expect of me? Pat thinks. *This morning I saw seven men being shot and lowered into a mass grave within the confines of the Glasshouse. Even in death they are not allowed to pass beyond its walls. A man would want to be more than a rock to deal with this – he would need to be a mountain.*

'You never asked me how things went this morning,' Pat says.

He has on a loose blue cotton vest, top buttons open, pyjama trousers and wine dressing gown that lies open. He had washed his hands and face in the ceramic bowl in his bedroom, but still feels unclean. He had taken the point of a small scissors to his fingernails and sliced under his thumb in his zeal to get rid of the earth he had that morning scooped up with

163

his bare hands and thrown on top of the coffins.

'I didn't have to quiz you – it was in your face and I heard from one of the firing party, a man I know …'

'I see.'

'Moore's knees gave way when he saw the blood and guts spattered about the post and on the wall behind him.'

'I think it was the smell more so than the sight.'

Of burst flesh, seared bone, shit and piss, shredded innards – a human abattoir.

'I was told he regained his composure quickly enough,' Kevin says.

'He did.'

'Now there's no more you can do for those lads, other than pray. You need to get back to yourself and help your parishioners, those left in this world.'

'I won't rest until their bodies are removed from that hellhole.'

Kevin sighs, says that the whiskey isn't helping his cold any, then mentions that Pat hadn't to worry – the families of the men won't rest until that happens.

'How did it go with the families this afternoon?' he asks in sudden afterthought.

'Badly. I called in to Father Swan to see would he come round with me, as he would know the families, where they lived, but he said he wasn't available, nor was there any priest available. I called to the Carmelite Church and Father Tony came with me. I got to see all the next of kin except for young White's mother, she wasn't in.'

Father Peter Swan, a quiet man, determinedly bitter.

'Tomorrow, then. Ignore the Swan boyo – he wouldn't forgive his own mother for burning porridge. Half that town is bitter tonight and the other half is celebrating.'

'You know him.'

'Unfortunately.'

'Enough said, so.'

'Aye. And of the families?'

'Need you ask? 'Twas a great scene of tragedy in every house we called to. They looked at me like I was telling them lies, and then the truth sank in and shock. Blame and accusations and the letters – silence when reading them. The grief was almost intolerable. Only for the friar, I doubt if I'd have been able to cope. I expect I'll see some of them again – they'll have questions for me – how was he in his last days, Father, did he suffer, when do you think they'll allow him home?'

'More than likely, you'll be talking to them all again – and you probably need to.'

'And you tell me it's over.'

That night, his colleague long retired, he pulls an easy chair up to the stove, drops several sods of turf in its belly, and sits in the dark. Images of the day torment him – the pale faces, faltering steps, the loud report of a half-dozen rifles, bodies washed by the medics in a tent and dressed, buried remains, speaking with the firing party afterwards, sombre men, shaken a little but not much. Theirs was a duty placed upon them by a government to which they had pledged allegiance.

It is permissible for them to kill during war.

Thou shalt not kill.

Addenda by the human race?

Except when it suits. Exigencies.

The knock on the front door is loud, filling the house with noise. He slides his feet into his carpet slippers, closes over his gown, loops its cord and goes to answer.

Father Kevin says from the top of the landing, 'It could be Private Flannery about his wife – she's dying. Show him into the study till I dress myself.'

But it is not Private Flannery. Although the man has his back to him, he knows the caller.

Kearney turns about and looks at Father Pat and says, 'We need to talk, Father, you and I. You've been bothering my mind.'

'Confession's tomorrow, in the church.'

'I'm not here to confess.'

'It's late, and I'm tired.'

'We're all tired, Father, but no rest for the wicked, isn't that what they say?'

'Fine, let's talk.'

The officer walks past him and waits halfway down the narrow hall. He smells of cologne and a wet coat.

Father Pat closes the door on the drizzle, the motor outside the gates.

'Head through into the kitchen,' he says.

Father Kevin calls from the landing, 'Is it …?'

'No, it's Captain Kearney.'

Pause.

'I'll leave youse to it, so.'

He shows the captain the table, the fiddleback chair closest to the potbelly.

'You'll have a drink?' Father Pat offers.

'Tea, black, two sugars.'

'Black tea – this is official business, is it?'

'Sort of, and a sort of filling you in on the lie of the land.'

'I saw enough disturbance of land today.'

The officer crosses his legs and removes a cigarette from a silver case. 'Father?'

Shake of head, wave of hand. The case is closed and the cigarette tapped against it, strike of match.

Father Pat busies himself with the making of tea. 'I'm afraid the jug has only got the scratchings of sugar.'

'I've had to do without more than a bit of sugar in my life.'

'Haven't we all, at one time or another, had to do without? So,' Father Pat says, sitting in the easy chair, regretting this because he thinks it gives the officer a slight advantage, looking down on him.

'So,' the officer says. A vein of blue smoke fogs the air. 'So, Father, do you like it here?'

'That's not a question to ask after the day of it.'

'Then I'll skip the small talk; I'm not one for it anyway.'

'To the point, good.'

'Did any of the men speak to you of Lieutenant John Wogan Browne?'

'Wogan Browne …'

No, not by name, he thinks. *Perhaps by sin? Yes – by sin.*

'You've heard of the name?'

'I have. I was serving in Dundrum when he was killed – Father Kevin only mentioned it to me in passing.'

'He was murdered.'

'You'd be an expert on that sort of thing.'

If the barb stings, it doesn't register on the officer's face. He remains as impassive as a circle stone.

'The question, Father, if you don't mind?'

'I do mind – what's said in the confessional is secret.'

'Outside of it …'

'No one said anything to me about Wogan Browne.'

The officer smokes his cigarette, eyeing the priest coolly. 'You know,' he says, 'we questioned them all in turn about that murder. We let the one go who told us something about the crime, who gave us a name.'

'Dooley?'

'We also freed young Hennigan – which of the two spoke up is *secret.*'

'Why are you here?'

'I'll come to that soon. You know, if the murderer had admitted to his crime, we'd have shot him and only him. We told him this and he said, "Fuck off with yourselves."'

'What about Behan – the witnesses to his murder?'

'Murder? He resisted arrest and was shot because he attempted to escape. Do you really think in the dark of the night people actually saw what happened? And do you honestly believe that the circumstances of Behan's death were a factor in deciding that the executions took place – to silence them? What of the troops under my command? Soldiers talk. Come now, the collar doesn't tighten the circulation to your head, does it?' Their eyes lock, neither flinching.

'Don't be insulting – this is not one of your privates you're addressing.'

The officer breaks eye contact, draws on his cigarette and rests it on the groove in the glass ashtray, sips at his tea.

'There's a history to what happened this morning. If you want to hear it, I'll tell you. If not, I'll be on my way … momentarily.'

The last word hangs like an empty noose, like something he has yet to fill and swing.

'To do with your late brother?'

'No, nothing to do with Paddy – he was killed in battle, finished off, but this has nothing to do with him.'

Said too positively for it to be totally true.

'Tell me. I'd love to know why eight men weren't shown a scrap of mercy.'

'Don't interrupt…'

He does as bidden.

He hears of Friday, 10 February – ten months ago.

Lt John Wogan Browne, a British officer, who called as usual to the Hibernian Bank in Kildare's main street to collect the wages for soldiers of his regiment in the artillery barracks, a five-minute walk down the Dublin road. As he walked back towards the barracks, there was a motorcar on the road, its hood raised, with three men paying attention to the engine. As the officer passed, one of the men pointed a revolver at him and demanded that he hand over the money. When he refused, he was shot through the forehead. He was an only son and his death outraged the British authorities and also Michael Collins, the Irish army's chief of staff. Winston Churchill, Secretary for the Colonies, cancelled all further withdrawal of British troops from Ireland until further notice. Collins dispatched a telegram to the secretary stating that he would do all in his power to bring the culprits to justice. Subsequently, three men were arrested but were later released. He ordered his army colleagues to discover who the perpetrators were and execute them – these were the chief of staff's last orders on the matter before he was killed in the ambush at Béal na Bláth.

There is almost silence when the officer finishes speaking, apart from the fall of turf in the stove, the tick of the grandfather clock.

'We're happy we got the man who squeezed the trigger,' Kearney says.

'Happy?'

'Satisfied, content – call it what you will.'

'There was no need to kill the others, so?'

'Oh, there was – they knew the murderer's identity but wouldn't give a name. They either lied or pretended that they didn't know.'

'Perhaps they genuinely didn't know.'

'They knew.'

'I know one who didn't, perhaps two, even three.'

'Why, because they didn't mention it to you?'

'I think they would have, if …'

'I'll never know – secrets of the confessional, eh?'

It was Moore who'd asked for forgiveness for killing a man in cold blood. No circumstances outlined, merely the silhouette of a bad deed. No name aired.

'Why did you consider it necessary to tell me all of this, Mr Kearney?'

'Because I thought you needed reminding about whose side you're on, about which side pays you your captain's salary – all you have to do to earn it is spread a few drops of water, say a few prayers and squander a few blessings on scum.'

'Scum? Squander?' His blood rises to boil.

'This morning – well, it was like a stitch in time saves nine.'

'Get out.'

Kearney moves quickly, pushes the priest in the chest, keeps his hand there, flat, pressing hard. Father Pat is taken by surprise – the man had been lightning quick, and he is strong, stronger than his slight frame suggests.

'Don't you ever fucking cross me again, or I swear

I'll stick a bullet in your fleshy head, Father. I've a fucking job to do and that's to make sure I deal with scum the way I'm told to do it. You fucking ever give me a sideways look again …'

He removes his hand and pulls down on the end of his tunic, adjusts his tie. His jaw is fixed hard. His teeth don't part when he speaks.

'I'll see myself out. So now you know why there's seven corpses in the Glasshouse, and they'll be staying there and you can tell that to those bastards in Kildare. But if one of them ever breathes my name, I'll come gunning for you. You're hardly a fucking man at all. A quivering fucking jelly of a man is all you are.'

For a long time, Father Pat can't bring himself to stir from the chair, and even though the stove is hot, it cannot warm the coldness he feels in his stomach, nor relax the grip of his hands on the armrests.

His eyes flicker open. The kitchen is in darkness. He listens to the wind breathe silent words of misery, a low wailing as doleful as he imagines any sound could possibly be. Yesterday's memories and those of last night vie for heed time in his mind, but he cannot bring himself to focus on any single thought or happening. Not yet.

Kevin must have looked in on him during the night, as a coat had been draped across his knees and the electric light turned off. He reckons he had fallen asleep sometime between three and four a.m., at a time when he was far from feeling sleepy. There was a shutdown in him, brought on by mental and physical exhaustion.

I'm tired, still, he thinks. *It's like I haven't slept for more than five minutes.*

His lower back is stiff and painful and he feels as though his soul had taken its leave of him, much like the heat had gone from the stove. It's what happens when someone turns one's blood cold.

A draught blows in under the back door, an invasive tongue of the wind.

This time yesterday it had yet to happen. That man, so much hatred in him – contained in the skin of a gentleman officer, one that likes another to think that the wearer had high ideals and high expectations of himself as well as of others, but he is no more than a true brute. What made him that way? There are no monsters in the cradle.

He is what he is.

He gets to his feet, holding his lower back, feels his way in the dark across the linoleum floor to the light switch and flips it on. Immediate light, the wonder of it. Next he opens the lip of the stove and sets a poker to the ashes, eases in one sod after another and thinks how it'll take time for the fire to catch hold, that perhaps it will be the same for him – it'll be a while before he will be able to take hold of himself, build up the fire.

That lad will come to a bad end, no doubt about it.

He goes to his room with a kettle of lukewarm water, shaves and washes his upper body. After this he lowers himself to his knees beside his bed and says his morning prayers, but that is all it is for him – a mere saying. His heart has distanced itself from the words and he acknowledges his God out of respect, politeness, even habit, understanding that he understands his maker less than he does Kearney.

He leaves a note on the kitchen table. He is taking the car to Kildare to speak with Mrs White. He had been about to write 'to break the news', but decided that the news had been long broken to her.

He wears a black coat and a blue scarf – he is prone to acquiring a sore throat and bad cold sores. Mrs Caulfield had told him that the friars in Kildare celebrated the feast day of St Blaise, who had a cure for the sore throat – might be worth getting the blessed oil and a scrap of the red flannel cloth.

'That'll fix the throat,' she said. 'I can get you a little liniment for the cold sores, but don't go kissing anyone meantime.' She says things that shouldn't be said after she's sampled the brandy or the altar wine.

What good would a saint's cure do you, a man of little faith?

It has the look of a dour day, wet and wild. He drives out of the camp along a treeless avenue, heading towards the main Dublin to Limerick road that passes through Kildare town. He does not like the Curragh. Too open, too bleak a landscape – what is there to see, only islands of furze bushes and sheep? Even the gold of the furze he had seen in late September when he first arrived in the Curragh did not unduly impress him. There was a breeze to the place. Even when the sun scorched the grass and farmers had to leave out troughs of water on the plains for the sheep and not a scrap of cloud blemished the sky, some class of wind was about to give him goose skin.

A warning?

The mountains to the east afforded the eye some beauty with their snowy caps and forests, but this treeless place was fit for soldiers and horse people and not much else. A place for coming to and leaving behind

– which he has made up his mind to do, though he realises that his mind had been halfway made up for
him. He does not dwell on this, this complete failing
of his courage.

He takes a left turn at Ballymany junction and tips
along a bumpy road. The round tower is in the distance, coming closer. A greyish, rather phallic-looking
object to have sticking at the air – and from within the
grounds of a cathedral, too. Not at all respectable.

He drives into a steep descent outside town, passes
a scattering of shabby cottages on the long stretch to
the town centre. He swings left at the market square.
The town is quiet, hardly anyone about.

Somewhere down here, he thinks, not fully sure but will
be once he sees the cottage, the wicket gate with the
missing slat near the parish church.

He finds the cottage easily enough. *As you do, he
thinks, whenever you would prefer a little delay when it came to
finding a place or a person. A little delay to bolster yourself, to
put off the inevitable, the dirty job.*

God, let me say the right words.

He knocks on the door, as he had done yesterday.
The smoke is heavy coming out of the chimney so he
knows she is inside, or someone is. He carries three
letters in his left hand.

He calls, 'Is anyone in?'

He hears movement. The top half of the door
opens to a crack.

Is this the woman? *Younger than I had thought.*

'Mrs White?'

'No, Father. Who'd be her, eh?' she says.

Another woman joins her. Ah, yes, he sees the boy in her. She has the face of someone who had lost a lot of weight owing to bad health or extreme and prolonged worry: black under her eyes, a triangle of wrinkles at the bridge of her nose, haggard and worn. Weathered, withered – near broken.

She says, 'It's okay, Sheila, you head off with yourself and thanks for everything – call back later, won't you? Tell the other women I want to be alone with the priest. Thanks for taking the boys with you. Be good for Sheila, won't youse? Good lads.' The boys go by him with heads lowered, not acknowledging his presence.

Boy chatter, indistinct, wooden gate closing out.

'Come in. Sit down by the fire, Father – you'll have tae?'

'I will, I will surely.'

'Sugar?'

'Two spoons.'

The house has the feel of a loving home. He'd been in others the last few days and weeks. The first thing he always noticed was the atmosphere – some had the comfortableness and assurance of love and others hadn't.

'I missed you yesterday, you were out when I called.'

She pours the tea, says she's sorry but she has nothing in to offer him to eat.

'I'm grand, not a bother.'

She sits almost opposite him after handing him a tin mug of tea.

'I was out front early yesterday. I heard the shots.'

'The noise carried this far?'

'We often hear the shots being fired on the ranges, the soldiers at practice. I never thought the day would come when I'd hear seven rows of shots breaking the air, one of them killing my son. Which row was he?'

'The first.'

Mention nothing of the coup de grace – a shot to the head for two of the lads. Unnecessary, though Buckley obviously thought otherwise.

'That's some comfort. The waiting must have played badly on the nerves of those waiting their turn. It took almost half an hour for the last shots to ring out.'

Forty-three minutes and thirty-five seconds, to be exact. Again, say nothing of this.

'It did … play badly on the nerves of a couple of the men.'

'So, Father, you've come to tell me news that I already know.'

'And to give you letters. I've brought some letters from Chalky.'

'Well, they're hardly letters of apology from the bastards who shot him.'

'I think you could live seven lifetimes and that might not happen.'

'I'd be waiting longer.'

She looks into the fire. He notices the wedding

band on her finger, and how worn her hands are. There's a pride in her and a real strength too. She wouldn't be one to run away from Kearney. *Not like someone else we know.*

'I was here yesterday when you called. I wanted to see no one, so no one was allowed across my threshold, neither you nor the parish priest. He'll never darken my door. You got to do it this once.'

'Chalky asked me to come see you – all the men asked that I should visit their folk, bring their letters and sit with ye a while.'

'In between sipping tae and licking up to the officers.'

'I drink tae and stronger than that with men from all walks.'

'You sit there, Father, and you tell me that it's right and proper for seven men to be shot dead and two of them only eighteen and one nine—' Breege breaks down, but is quick to compose herself.

'It wasn't right or proper.'

'It was murder.'

'The act is a stain on us, a stain on the soul of the country. As is the murder of Wogan Browne ...' His words trail off. *Tiptoeing to the official side now, are we – again? Coward of cowards, that's you, bucko, to a tee.*

'It was grown men who did that. And let me tell you something else – the boyos who did the killing aren't dead – they hopscotched it to Athlone and joined the Free State army. There's one for you. You didn't know that, did you?'

Who do I believe?

Breege says, 'Chalky was eighteen – what did he know about life, only what he learned from listening to gobshites.'

'He believed in his cause and he paid the price for choosing to believe in it.'

'I don't think he ever kissed a girl. I'll never see his smile. I've had a son stolen on me. Praying to Jesus Christ I was, night and day, for his eyes to open and for his thoughts to turn from running with the Volunteers. A waste of breath, praying.'

'He bore up well, Mrs White. There was no unsteadiness, no nerves in him – he loved you and his brothers and he loved his short life, and he was certain of his mother's love for him. That's all I know. Any man would have been glad to have had him as a son.'

'Do you think I don't know my own son? No nerves, Father? Don't lie – he used to sweat up over little arithmetic exercises that Brother Matthew set him.'

'It was quick.'

'Aye, his life went too quick.'

'The letters …' he says.

She takes them and puts them in her apron pocket. 'You never touched your tea, Father.'

'I've had about fourteen cups this morning. I've tea coming out my ears.'

'And words out of your arse.'

This stung him – its coarseness, directness, undiluted honesty. How many women would dare speak to a priest in such fashion? Very few, perhaps not enough. Remarkable woman, remarkable courage.

'I'll be leaving. If you want to ask me about your boy, how he was the last days, what he spoke of …'

'I want nothing from you now, Father, only your absence from my home. Go and be with your own kind.'

He nods. Sighing, he rises to his feet and puts his cup on the edge of the table.

'Before you go, Father, read this, from today's *Irish Independent*. Mr Wilson brought it down from Dublin this morning.'

'I didn't bring my glasses.'

'Sure, I'll read it for you.' She pitches her voice an octave higher. '"Four men in Kerry were tried for being in possession of guns and ammunition and received the death sentence, but this was suspended when they gave an oath not to attack Free State troops." They got off with a warning while my son was shot. What's the differ, Father?'

'Mercy and common sense prevailed.'

And Collins did not ask for their heads.

'Will you answer me something about all of this, Father?'

'If I can, I will.'

'Was my Chalky asked to give an oath like the one those boys made?'

'No.'

'How about Dooley and Hennigan?'

'I know nothing about them or if there's any truth in what's being said of them.'

181

'One last thing. You've other news for me, Father?'

'Other news, Mrs White?'

'When is Chalky coming home?'

'Have the other families not told you?'

'I want you to tell me.'

'They're buried in a yard in the Glasshouse.'

'They can't even find it in their hearts to give us our sons to bury?'

'When the war is over, I'm sure.'

'They're worse than the Black and Tans ever were, worse than the English.'

''Tis much stated that we Irish were always crueller to our own kin and kindred than any invader ever was.'

'The next time you're sipping tea with your Free State officers, tell them I said they're nothing only heartless murderers. Could you bring the cup from your lips long enough to say that, Father?'

'I will.'

He says this, though he knows he'll say no such thing.

She does not show a sign of getting up to see him out. He crosses to the door, looks back and says, 'I'm very sorry, Mrs White.'

'Father?' she says, not looking at him.

'Yes?'

'Thank you for bringing the letters.'

'No need.'

'Goodbye, Father.'

And it is goodbye, he thinks, in the motorcar, heading down towards Tully and the Japanese Gardens, taking another route to the Curragh. He will ask Kevin to put a word in with the bishop. A move will happen quickly enough, he is sure. A captain's salary, after all – better than a priest's usual stipend. For that money there are a goodly number of priests who wouldn't mind the squandering of a few blessings or wasting drops of holy water or staying on the right side of the wrong side.

Breege

In his immediate absence, she regrets being hard on the priest. He'd the cut of a friendly man about him and seemed severely at odds with himself. He reminded her of a crystal glass vase she had seen in a display cabinet in the Medlicott mansion on Dunmurry Hill, carrying a fracture as thick as the vein in the back of her hand – it was a mystery to her how the vase was holding itself together.

It is in her when she hears the closing of the motorcar's door to rush out and apologise to him, to bring him back in for a sip of brandy, to hear what he had to say about her son. To try and believe in his exaggerations, his niceties, to allow him speak, to listen to the last kindly and comforting voice her son had heard.

But she is too late – she hears the motorcar leave, the noise of its engine recede.

She had been thinking on it, but is acutely aware that when it came to the hunt, the priest could have camped outside her door for two nights and she still wouldn't have gotten up off her arse. All he has is bet feelings – no blood on his hands, the loss of no one.

Heal himself, he will – God looks after his own. They say. Like feck, He does.

She realises too that even if she'd spoken with him in the Curragh, he could have done nothing to save Chalky's life. Wilson had tried, had gone to Naas to visit George and asked him to pull a few strings with his well-connected friends. But he said the way things were, with government TDs being assassinated and Collins's death, no one was in the mood for listening – the mood was for bloodletting.

She half-rises and brings a small framed oval portrait from the mantelpiece to her lap, studies it. It's not right, not fair for a mother to have to bury her children.

She opens the envelope addressed to her and glances at the photograph before resting her eyes on the page, the crease as sharp as a blade in it. She reads, a tear falling on the page.

18 December 1922

Dear Mother,

I am writing these last few lines to you. By the time you receive this letter, it will all be over and so I ask you be strong, Mother, for little Anto and Seanie. I am to be executed tomorrow morning. I have been to confession and Holy Communion. Father – said we will go straight to Heaven. I have a few pounds in my suitcase, you can have them. I am sorry I ever got involved in all of this, as it is not worth it. Tell the boys to never get involved in this business. I wish to bid you goodbye and ask you to pray for me and the rest of the boys in here. Tell Anto and Seanie to pray for me.

Your loving son,
Chalky

'Chalky,' she says, clutching his photograph and his letter to her bosom, saying his name again in a rush of silently falling tears.

We slip into the hall at the rear of the Carmelite Church like we are stealing into some place forbidden. In a way, we are. There are people already inside and there I was, thinking we had left early enough to be the first to arrive, or at least among the first. But we are the last. I smell damp clothes, perfume, brilliantine and overriding these is one of paraffin used to fill two oil lamps that rest on tables and light up the hall and throw shadows on the walls and ceiling. The walls are distempered green above and the lower part is boarded, with the wood painted white, like a snug in any of the town's public houses. People look at us and say nothing. Some nod, a couple smile lukewarm smiles. It is Wilson who says hello for our small party – that lad would shake hands with the devil himself and his mother and be relaxed in their company, too. Like an overfriendly guard dog. The atmosphere is brittle, easily broken. I sense anger, frustration, shock – we blame ourselves, we blame each other, we blame someone else for having led our son to his grave.

Kin of the murdered, trying to sort out among ourselves what we ought to do, for we are at a loss.

Mrs Mangan dresses a small trestle table in a corner of the hall and on it we put vases of flowers, lighted votive candles, photographs of our dead sons and the goodbye letters each one wrote. Wilson tells Anto and Seanie where to sit and shushes them when they start to elbow each other in the ribs.

All the letters are more or less the same in style and content. A few lines of regret, of saying they are not afraid to die, that they had gladly fought for old Ireland, for brothers and sisters to take care of parents, proud to die for the Cause they'd loved and honoured.

Wilson whispers in my ear that there is no marked difference in them.

I whisper, 'How many ways are there of bidding farewell?'

It's not lost to me that the priest's name had been omitted from the letters, and that in a few instances the men state that Father ———— sends his prayers and sympathies. I take this as an indication that it was not intended for him to visit the bereaved – he must have taken it on his own bat and had probably got into trouble for doing so. But perhaps not – his superiors would have seen him doing the rounds of the homes as something that would make life hard for him, and probably thought, 'Let him off with himself.' Still, I don't have an ounce of pity in me for him. Which doesn't say anything good about me.

Christmas had passed us by, the New Year too, coming and going in a blur.

1923. This will be a year of first anniversaries.

Only for Wilson I think I would have caved in on myself. He has been remarkably kind – when you've had a husband who'd been remarkably unkind, then you are quick to notice the difference. You see it in the little things: taking the boys away when I am in no mood for them, when there is a risk I might say something or lash out at them for no reason, harsh words and actions they might be slow to forgive and never forget. They are too young to understand that my anger and frustration is not with them, but with Chalky.

The hall is full of chatter that falls to silence when Father Tony comes in. We appreciate his saying Mass – if Father Swan found out, he would do all in his power to prevent it taking place. In his eyes and that of the bishops, our boys had put themselves outside the Church by fighting against the Free Staters, their pals.

But there is always a rebel in every walk of life, someone who will do bad for a good reason.

I can't say this of Chalky; he was too indecisive about which side to join and he should have done what many others did, which was to keep his nose out of the war. Lads like Chalky joined the National Army but then deserted and ended up being shot for treachery. It's a fact of life that some people just don't know when and where to turn and when not to, and it gets them and others killed.

The Mass is lovely. The friar calls out the names of our boys, includes Thos Behan, who he says was a fine poet and reads an extract from a poem of his called 'My Calico Shack in Kildare' about his capture and his internment in the Rath Camp on the Curragh in 1921. I can tell by looking at their faces that some of the women are annoyed with the friar; he'd spent too much time talking about Behan, one man.

Why is my son not entitled to the same quantity of time? Behan had his funeral.

Father Tony is alert to this, however, and has the good sense to realise that time, while no longer of importance to the dead, remains important for the living – and their dead. So he moves on, reciting all the names again.

'Holy Father in Heaven, bless …'

I like the smell of burning incense and candle smoke, but paraffin gives me a blinding headache, especially when the mantle has just been lit and it gives off smoke.

We are tidying the hall after the Mass and the subsequent meeting. Letters will be written to politicians and the religious hierarchy requesting the return of our loved ones. Constant badgering, demanding, threatening, a refusal to accept their treatment of our loved ones as nothing less than murder, and also their cruel treatment of us.

Ours are not theirs to keep.

There is fire and hope in me as I walk home with Wilson in the first snowfall of winter. The boys have run on ahead. I am filled with resolve and purpose and though I dislike a few of the other parents and would not be caught in their company under normal circumstances, I am glad we are lending steel to each other.

Wilson is quiet. The collar of his coat is raised, the soft peak of his cap deep over his eyes. He is taller than me. He keeps my hand in his coat pocket – in daylight, he walks beside me with a gap. His hand is warm. I feel with my thumb the place where he used to have knuckles – a kick from a horse smashed three to fragments.

'What's on your mind?' I say.

'Nothing.'

But I sense that there is. 'Out with it, Wilson.'

'I've been thinking …' His words trail off. The snow is falling hard, swarm of communion hosts, staying on the ground to form a plush white carpet.

'About?' I push.

'What we might do down the line …'

Is he thinking of marriage? At a time like this? I don't know whether I should feel vexed or pleased. Or downright bloody hurt.

'And what do you think it is we might do?'

We cross the road at the bottom of the hill – the long and narrow street is empty. A pair of fresh tyre tracks in the snow.

'I've been thinking about this for an age – about emigrating.'

'Emigrating?' I remove my hand.

'I mean all of us – the four of us.'

'You've been thinking about this at a time like this? When my son is buried in a plot in—'

'A fresh start …'

I'm furious and increase my pace to make it plain that I do not want to be in his company. He lingers and then runs to catch up, almost slipping on the snow, which would have been a funny sight to me if the moment was different.

'Breege!' he pants. 'We need to start a new life – not here. Me, you, the lads – we can get married. Move away from this fucking place after the funeral.' He stops trying to keep up with me.

I turn to look at him. He stands several feet away from me. I want to kiss him and slap his face at the same time.

Instead, I say, 'I don't know where my mind is at. Go home, Wilson. Leave me alone for a few days. Just go.'

He knows me well enough to know when there's no talking to me and he turns and walks away. But he does not walk too far and I see him out of the corner of my eye when I open the wicket gate, that he'd followed me at a distance to see that I'd gotten safely home.

Inside, it is Anto who asks, pausing during the lighting of candles. 'Where's Wilson?'

'He'd to go home.'

Seanie says, 'Were ye fighting?'

'No, we weren't fighting.'

'I heard ye fighting.'

'Seanie, we were not fighting.'

'I'm hungry, Ma,' Anto says. He's always hungry.

If not for food, it's for attention.

'It's not "Ma" – Ma is what sheep say, and aren't you a quare-looking sheep?'

Before he or Seanie can edge in a word, there is the thud of a book falling upstairs.

I don't think any of us will ever forget that moment.

Kearney

It was like a knife had been stuck in his gut when told that Bergin had been observed running messages for the Irregulars interned in Tintown. He'd bet a week's wages with Buckley that he was wrong about the corporal. But there you have it – you can trust very few. One in twelve, Christ might say.

'You're absolutely certain?' Kearney says, looking sidelong at Buckley.

'Positive.'

They are sitting at the bar in Ceannt officers' mess in the Curragh. Plush, fawn-carpeted, a log fire blazing, other officers sitting at round tables, blue haze of pipe and cigarette smoke. A buzz of conversation, small laughter. Bergin had been a barman in the mess up to six months ago, a polite young man who had worked in a Dublin hotel and came from a good background. Jesus, Kearney thinks, the man had smiled and assented approval with a nod during a late-night session in the mess, after the executions last year, when I said, *That'll settle their cough. They won't be doing any more sniping at our lads.*

'And that's for sure, Sir,' he had said.

That's typical of that shower – stab you in the back, lie, cheat, rob.

'I pushed his name forward for promotion,' Kearney says, staring at the cap of froth on his beer.

'So did I,' Buckley says. 'More fool the two of us.'

Buckley nurses a whiskey glass, fires the dregs down his throat, gestures with the glass to the barman, 'A double.' Drums his thick fingers on the varnished counter.

Kearney sighs and looks across the floor at his commanding officer, trying to catch his eye.

'What are you at?' Buckley says.

'That bollocks needs to be taught a lesson.'

'Who, the boss?'

'Not the boss, you fucking jennet.'

Buckley laughs. 'Settle in yourself, will you?'

He sniffles, raises his bushy fair eyebrows. 'Aye – but you'd nearly be heartsick of dishing out the lessons.'

'So what do we with a traitor?'

'I said nearly heartsick.'

'Ah, Conor …'

Lt Colonel Costello excuses himself from his table and joins Kearney and Buckley at the counter.

'Gentlemen?' he says, fixing his gaze on Kearney.

'Sir,' he says, 'we've just received some intelligence concerning …'

The solemn head nods, face darkening with each word of Kearney's.

'Okay. Sort it out. If you find documentation …'

'Transport, Sir?' Buckley says.

'Leave that with me – I'll get on to the duty trans-port NCO in Clarke Barracks. He'll issue you with a car.'

They drink to fortify themselves against the night chill and discuss who they might use as a driver.

'I know a good man,' Buckley says. 'Higgins. The Irregulars shot his best friend, and naturally he's a bit-ter shite for it. If he's around, we'll get him.'

'What time should we move?'

Buckley glances at the clock on the glass shelf above the wall mirror behind the bar and says, 'He's going with a yoke in Kildare – he should be cycling in the Rath road in about two hours, carrying the smell of her on his fingers and letters for the boys in his shirt pocket.'

'Call me,' Kearney says.

'Where are you going?'

'To lie down for a while.'

He slides from the barstool and reaches for his pint and takes a last swallow.

'You know the date it is?' Buckley says.

'I do.'

'A quick year, wasn't it?'

'Yes, a quick year all right.'

In his single room on the second floor of the mess, he lights a candle and sits on the wide windowsill. Smokes. His room smells of furniture polish and he reminds himself to thank Polly for putting in the ef-fort in and out of the bed. *She'll make someone a good wife. Not me, though. I'd prefer a woman who's a little better looking and isn't as practised as Polly – where did she learn those things, tucking her heel into the cheek of my arse to bring more of me into her? But then, she's been working in the officers' mess for what, five or six years?* Well poked by the time he'd started on her, no doubt.

She's friendly with Mrs Caulfield, the priests' housekeeper. Between that pair no secret has a chance of being lost between the cracks. They gossip the night away, which is useful if a man would like to spread a lie around or if he wants to listen in without making it obvious that he is. He sieves for the truth, bits and pieces of information that sometimes add sense to the bits and pieces he already owns.

Father Pat Donnelly, up in a remote, obscure parish in Donegal. The nerves came at him badly.

If he had kept to himself and not become em-broiled with condemned men, there wouldn't be a bother in him. They weren't condemned for no rea-son, or on a whim. A good job was done. Kildare is quiet since the executions, not a shop raided since and the trains aren't being attacked. And people who wanted revenge for a murder were happy with the end result. He supposes that they were like people who, having complained of meagre portions on their din-ner plates, were then given too much to digest. He'd changed the air in Kildare, all right.

A quick year, no doubt. A year ago this evening,

they had rounded up the rat column at Moore's Bridge.

In a war, he thinks, only the brutal do well. *And in peacetime, too*, breathes a different inner voice.

The families want the bodies back. He no longer has a say, as he'd been permanently transferred to Intelligence. The Governor of the Glasshouse says they'll have to wait until the war is over, and maybe then he'll turn his thoughts to their requests. Till then … Fair fucks to him for standing his ground. He lifts the sash window and flicks his cigarette stub outside, shuts the window. Watches the eye of the cigarette die on the wet ground and then allows his pinch of net curtain to fall into place.

Thinks of his brother. Travelling along the road, his thoughts on what? His fiancée, most likely. Paddy was always the dreamer, born soft-hearted. Next thing, round a bend, into an enfilade of fire from .303 Lee Enfields and shotguns. The walk-up then, the coup de grace – he was alive, a witness said, a middle-aged tinker who'd put his eye to the hedge. 'Alive, Sur, and begging for his life, but yer man just put the gun to his head and that was it for him, Sur. A bad bastard, Sir, bad bastard. The heart lepped sideways in me with the fright.'

Though he had tried to determine the identity of his brother's killer, he wasn't successful. But this does not matter to him now, for each Irregular he kills or tortures is his brother's killer.

One of these days, all this will end. His services

will be no longer required – the dirty work service for the top nobs.

What then?

Time to think about that when then arrives.

He moves to the bed and kicks off his shoes and lies down, the green anti-back riding up in a ridge under his back. Such a headache, ripping his forehead apart.

The growth of a conscience?

'A conscience,' he murmurs.

The first living creature he had killed was a black-and-white mongrel pup. He had hanged it from a tree with binder twine, just to see how it died and to explore the difference between the two beings – the being alive, the being dead. Paddy had chanced across the scene in the small clearing behind their cottage and ran scream-ing to their father, who hurried along to see with his own eyes. By the time he arrived, he'd gone to the river with the dead pup and so his father never got to see the result and therefore the fullness of his 'bad deed'.

In the kitchen, he belted him across the arse with his folded trouser belt and lugged him by the ear to con-fession. As if confession would bring back their pup.

The church was empty. There were flowers on the altar, lots of them. He must have been only eight or nine back then. Twenty-five years ago. He had never been in an empty church before and he quite liked it, the stillness, the serenity. As they walked to the front of the church, the din from his father's hobnailed soles reached the high-vaulted ceiling, disturbing the tranquillity, bothering, he was sure, the figurines in the bas-relief of Roman soldiers and Christ stumbling toward martyrdom and resurrection.

His father put him in a pew opposite a confessional booth, ordered him to stay there, and went and fetched a priest. A balding silvery-haired man called Father O'Connor who people were jealous of because his parents had left him plenty of money and who Father liked because he was educated, like him.

The two men spoke in hushed tones under a framed portrait of an evil-looking Christ. Once he'd sat in a pew closest to the portrait at noon Mass and swore that the eyes of the Christ were staring at him in a glassy-eyed, penetrating stare. His mother was gone a year – had moved to London with a vet who lived down the road. The priest approached and motioned for him to enter the confessional. He went in and knelt and waited for the wooden panel to slide back from the grille.

When it did he released his words. 'Bless me Father, for I have sinned – it's a month since my last confession.'

'And what are your sins?'

'I killed a pup.'

'Why?'

There was no reason, but he could not say this. He searched for a way to make the sin less of a real sin.

'She was always getting sick and in pain.'

'And she was a pup from your mother's dog?'

'Yes.'

'And how did that dog die?'

'Don't know, Father – we think it ate poison.'

'I see. And why did you hang the pup?'

He had considered cutting her throat, but he didn't want to clean up a mess of blood. And anyway, hanging held more appeal. He had overheard the bigger lads in the village saying it was great craic – they'd hung a cat at Hallowe'en.

'I don't know, Father.'

'Are you sorry you did this act?'

He wasn't but he said he was.

'So I could trust you with my pup if I left him with you to mind?' *You could in your hole, Father.*

'Yes.'

'You wouldn't hang him?'

'No.'

'You're sure?'

'Yes, Father.' Kearney smelled stale whiskey and bad feet.

'What was your dog's name?'

'Charlie.'

Penance amounted to ten Hail Marys and ten Our Fathers. A stiff fine.

They park off road a little, close to a derelict shack, one of many in the abandoned Rath camp, still in the process of dismantlement, selling off what is worth selling before demolition. The engine is off. North-west, fifty yards distant, lies the deserted main Dublin road.

'He's late,' Buckley says.

Higgins the driver hasn't said much. The worry with quiet men is that you don't know what's keeping them quiet.

'You're away tomorrow, Art,' Buckley says, nerves on his tongue.

'In the afternoon.'

'Wales is nice.'

'It is. I need the week's rest.'

Higgins says, looking over his shoulder, 'What part of Wales, Sir?'

'Cardiff.'

'I have a sister there, lives down Albany Road.'

'Jay! There you are, Art – a holiday and a ride,' Buckley says.

'Ah, I don't think so, Sir. Emily is seventy-nine.'

'There's always a bloody catch, isn't there?' Buckley says.

Art says, 'I'll say nothing if she says nothing.'

Back to keeping secrets…

Higgins laughs, but it is a distinctly unhappy sort of laugh.

A light …

'This fucking has to be him,' Buckley says.

'I hope so,' Kearney says.

Thus far, at intervals they'd stopped three cyclists: two soldiers and a prostitute called Alice Donovan, who he had visited once in her sister's house. Not a bad little filly at all to have under you. Compliant and not objectionable about which orifice you used. Higgins said she was to pedal back to Kildare and then she said was going to see someone important and breathed a name and they let her through, a high-ranking officer not he nor many others would want to cross, not even when he was having a good day.

Higgins gets out and takes the oil lamp from the seat beside him, pumps the lever to bring up the light and goes and stands in the middle of the road. Buckley steps onto the grass verge. The whirring of the bike's wheels, closer and closer, its light bobbing, weaving this side to the other when avoiding potholes. The tiniest screech of brakes, sound of a boot scuffing the road to aid the brake.

Panting, the exertive breathing of a fit young man.

'What's your name, soldier?' Buckley says, walking to the rear of the bicycle.

'Bergin, Sir, Corporal Bergin.'

'I can see your fucking rank markings, soldier. Didn't I help putting the fucking things there, you unappreciative cur.'

Higgins says, 'Stand away from the bike and put your hands behind your head.'

Bergin eases the bike to the ground and straightens up.

'Hands on your head, before I fucking nail them there for you,' Buckley says.

Kearney steps from the shadows and says in the friendliest tone he can muster, 'My friends here insist that you're running messages for the boys in Tintown and I've wagered a week's wages against them that it's not true.'

Bergin is tall and thin, with an unusually long neck. It runs like a pipe from an oversized shirt collar.

'Is it?'

Bergin looks at the ground.

'Buckley – search him.'

Buckley dives his hand into an inside pocket and brings a sheaf of papers to the surface. He slaps them across Bergin's face. 'Bastard!' He hands them to Kearney, who reads a couple, bringing them close to the lamp. Squints.

'I've lost, it seems. I lose, you lose.'

Bergin kicks out at the oil lamp but misses.

Kearney points at him with his revolver and fires once, twice. When Bergin falls to the ground, he stands over him and looses two more bullets into the body. He kicks the face. Once, twice – a snap of bone.

'Jesus!' Higgins says.

'For the loving lamp of Jasus,' Buckley says, pulling at Kearney's arm, 'come away off him, for fuck's sake – there's a time and a place.'

Higgins drops to his knee, examines Bergin. 'He's still breathing.'

'Bring him to the car.'

Buckley and Higgins look at each other and the latter hands the lamp to Kearney. They ease Bergin into the back of the car.

'Fucker's bleeding like a stuck pig,' Higgins says.

Kearney says to Higgins, 'Get the bike off the road and bring his cap along and anything else that the cunt dropped.'

Kearney extinguishes the lamp and says to Higgins, 'Bring us to a quiet road, by the canal.'

'Sir.'

The car lurches forward, takes to the main road, turns right and then travels for a mile where Higgins goes left, up by the back of the Main Stand at the Curragh Racecourse, passing the boreen leading to the Fen and veering right, travelling over Moore's Bridge that bends a little halfway.

'Where are we off to?' Buckley says, wiping his lips after a swig of whiskey, returning the flask to Kearney, who gulps a swallow and offers the flask to Higgins, who polishes off the contents.

Kearney says, 'Just before the bridge in Milltown, there's a dirt road, okay?'

Higgins nods. About ten minutes later, a short distance in on the dirt road, Kearney says, 'Stop here.'

Alighting, he says, 'Bring that fucker around the back -- we'll give him a ride that he won't forget. One of a lifetime.'

They tie Bergin's wrists to the rear fender and drag him along the stony road, no one saying a word during the journey.

Buckley says, 'That's enough – that's long enough. Leave them some of his face to look at.'

Kearney says, 'There's no distance long enough for his sort.'

But he signals for Higgins to stop driving. They get out and cut the body free.

Kearney says, 'I think we can say that's a job well done.'

'Now what?' Buckley says.

'Fuck him into the canal. The water will clean him up a bit,' Kearney says.

Buckley and Higgins pick up the broken body and throw it into the waters, amongst the rushes. Higgins is about to fling in the man's bloodstained cap when Kearney says, 'No, no – that's a present for someone.'

Higgins says, 'A present?'

Buckley says, 'Haven't we done enough?'

'One more thing. I'll do it.'

A little going away present.

Breege

Wilson says to me, ''Tis worse this country is getting.'

I do not respond. He has not spoken outright to me of emigrating since the night of the Mass, many months ago. But he likes to hint or allude to it whenever the opportunity presents itself, no matter how vaguely, to remind me that he has not given up on the idea. I used to think these hints were figments of my imagination, but there's been too many instances for my mind to be concocting things. It's definitely in his mind to shift the lot of us to new sod.

'Pour the tea, Wilson, and make yourself useful.'

'Throwing the cap into the girlfriend's hall – it soaked in blood – her screams woke people up along the entire row of houses.'

'Yes, sheer awful.'

'And the night that was in it too, eh?'

I cut thin slices of brown bread and say, 'How many?'

'Two is grand – any cheese left?'

'Any amount of cheese. Bring the butter with you.'

He crosses to the larder and on his return journey he says, 'Where're the lads?'

'Next door.'

He sits down at the table, rubs his hands together and blesses himself.

'They found the body in the canal at Milltown,' he says.

I butter the bread.

'Beaten to a pulp and shot, I was told,' he says.

'God love him.'

'Aye, God love him.'

Nothing is said for a few moments. He feigns interest in the small window close to the door. The net curtain has been removed for the wash and he can see through the clear, clean window the stone flower trough on the sill, the ribby sapling in the centre of the garden, the privet hedging that borders the garden from the road. Pleasant skies this morning, sunny. Looking at the scene could fool you into leaving the cottage without a coat, but the sharp air would divide the bones in you.

Turning to me, he says, 'The police are hopping mad, the people too – people are losing faith in the National Army.'

'What faith?' I snap.

'Well, you'd expect them fellas, if they're going to be representative of us, to have high ideals, not to be going around plugging people, taking the law into their own hands. That has to end.'

'Has it, will it?' I bite on a slice of bread. Yes, as good as Mother used to bake.

'If we're to stay here, it must surely.'

I swallow, count to ten in my mind. Him and his hints. 'And when are you off?' I say.

This lad needs a bit of play.

'As soon as I've eaten this,' he looks at me with hope. 'Unless you've something you'd like me to do?'

'No, not that I can think of at this moment.'

Hope flags and withers in his eyes. Up with my skirt? He has high hopes with the mood he's after putting me in.

'And I was meaning about you emigrating. Won't you send us a postcard?'

The face on him. Talk about grim.

'Won't you not forget?'

'I won't forget,' he says.

When he is gone, I freshen my cup. I hear the voices of children at play in Sheila's back garden. Eddie had fixed up a swing for them and sure, you'd think they'd never seen one before. Kicking a ball about too. Last night – a year ago last night – Moore's Bridge, the dug-out, the talk at the gate, my last with my eldest son. Not realising it then, but living the fear of it every time my eyes lost sight of him. And now, another death – a brutal one too – no less, no more brutal than Chalky's, but at least the Bergin chap appears to have got it smartly and wasn't left hanging on for days, hoping against hope, longing for a miracle of mercy from a crowd of vainglorious bastards who wanted the smell of blood in their nostrils. Who'd want a pining death?

Chalky has not come home. He lies there with the

others in a prison grave. Letters written to here, there and everywhere – pleas made on the families' behalf by eminent people, falling flat like stones in a pond.

Too soon.

Not yet.

Wait until the first anniversary has passed. We'll review matters then. When there's a marked decrease in violence.

No progress, then little progress, not much. It's when, not if, whereas before they'd come up against a wall of silence.

Another few pushes and hearts not used to giving might give a little, in the spirit of reconciliation. No, not reconciliation – never that – appeasement, isn't that the big word the committee's solicitor used? Appease, make us quiet. Shut us up.

Kearney

He steps onto the platform at Kildare train station, dressed in civilian attire, shoulders a little hunched, weighted with fatigue. Washy complexion from a rough sea crossing; he'd emptied his guts into the inshore green of the Irish Sea, which had left a taste of beer vomit in his mouth and aching ribs from having heaved so hard. He had stayed on deck for much of the night, away from the roughhouse bar, the bawdy singing, hung away in the manner of a bad soul avoiding the light. It wouldn't be the first time an Irish officer was recognised by hard necks and dumped over the railing into the sea. Who is to tell what happened to Lieutenant Sean Humphries? He fell overboard – death by accident, suicide or murder? Accident, they'd decided. Convenient. His own source, a republican by the name of Froggy Dunne, told him that Humphries had fought like a lion to save himself, but he was disarmed before he could use his pistol.

He walks up and down the platform, looking for Buckley. Not a sign of him. The train hasn't been delayed – where the fuck is he? Outside?

Passing through the archway, he looks at his watch. The oblong spread of gravel is empty of motorcar,

horse and ass and their carts in the encroaching darkness. The few passengers who had alighted are heading for town in dribs and drabs, all in a hurry; in their
heads they are already at home. A mother, two boys
and a wiry man one boy called Wilson, thanking him
for the day out in Dublin. She stares at him for milliseconds, as if something about him is familiar. She's
attractive in the way of some women who fall short of
being pretty, but who make up for it in charm and an
appeal no one has yet put a name to. Then she looks
away, taking a bothered look with her.

His mind works on what he ought to do. Walk to
Bang-Up Lane off the square and hire a motorcar?
*No, just in case someone recognises me... Had the woman?
From a checkpoint she had passed through? Hardly, though –
the moustache is gone, I'm out of uniform and capless. In the
dimming light, it'd be difficult to identify me, and even if it did
happen – well, it's fifty-fifty odds as to whether my hand would
be shaken or my head presented with a bullet.*

For reassurance, he feels the grooved walnut hand-
grip of his Webley revolver in his trench coat's inside
pocket. *Wait a few more minutes. It's not as if you're in a
desperate hurry to be anywhere – you're not keeping a firing
party waiting, are you?* He hears the engine before he
sees the car round the bend and straighten for him.

About bloody time.

Buckley pulls up alongside him. 'Get in, quick.'

His friend wears a troubled expression. He puts his
suitcase in the back and gets in the car, staring at his
colleague with a puzzled frown.

'What's up?' he asks.

Buckley's gloved hand comes up. 'In a minute.'

He turns left and drives over a railway bridge, passing a stables, coming to a Y junction a mile out where he hangs right.

It is dark a few minutes later when the headlamps face in the direction of the Curragh Camp, three miles distant by road, two by foot. On a sunny summer's day from here, Little Curragh, the view is splendid; yellow gorse, the grey parapet walls of Moore's Bridge, its large semi-circle eye of tunnel, in the immediate background the green and blues of the Wicklow Mountains and draped above these a long frill of white cloud and the tiniest slivers of blue.

Without warning, Buckley pulls over and reverses into a driveway, engine sputtering but not conking out.

'You're better off hearing this from me,' Buckley says.

'For God's sake, will you spit it out?'

'The police are wanting to speak with you – about Bergin. They've already had words with myself and Higgins. We told them nothing.'

'I'll tell them the same.'

'They suspect you of killing Noel Lemass and Timmy Rodgers.'

'So? Come on. Suspecting and proving are horses of different colours. Are you losing your nerve, Buckley?'

'I'm trying to stay ahead of things.'

'We are?'

'The manner of Bergin's death has the politicians and the generals asking questions – the likes of questions they didn't ask us before. They're singing from the same hymn sheet on this one, Art – the Irregulars and our lot.'

Kearney sighs, touches his sore tooth with the tip of his tongue, enjoying the small pain. He sighs again, long and hard. He accepts the cigarette proffered by Buckley, and the light.

Buckley coughs, dabs the back of his hand to his nostrils, says, 'The thing is this – you could be court-martialled. You could be staring at a noose for this, Art, or a firing squad.'

'That's bull.'

'It's not – Costello will tell you there's been a change of wind.'

'A change of fucking wind?'

'Aye. And you better wake up to the seriousness of this – there's pressure coming from on high for you to be court-martialled for Bergin's murder.'

'Me? Alone?'

'You did the shooting, boy.'

'And you haven't done that before.'

'I did, when I was told to do it. No one ordered you to take out Bergin. And besides, it's your name the top dogs in the Irregulars are barking, the police too – it's cropped up too many times.'

'You better bring me to see Costello.'

'Okay, but I told you nothing about this, so act surprised.'

'Do you think he's stupid? He'll know you tipped me off.'

'Just act surprised anyway.'

'I won't have to act – I'll be surprised for days at this. Silly bastards trying to get justice for a rat, a traitor. The only justice for his kind is the sort I meted out.'

'The simple fact is this, Art – they don't need men like us any more.'

Buckley adds that it's not to the Curragh they're going, but the CO's house in Newbridge.

'The redcaps are waiting for you to show.'

The Costello home is off Eyre Street, the town's one-sided main street. It has an ivy-covered façade, red-brick gables, like the houses in the Camp.

Costello is sharper and meaner in his delivery than Buckley. He said Art had burned the arse out of the pan this time. Six months ago this could have been smoothed over – another terrible atrocity in a glut of them by both sides – but this is not six months ago and there is no glut and minds are focused on this. After speaking, he moves to the long window with a letter opener, using the handle end to prise out a thumbtack embedded in the frame.

Then he returns to his desk and sits down. Kearney says, sitting straight backed on a chair facing the intelligence officer, 'What do you propose I should do?'

'I have a brother in Buenos Aires. I think you should leave for there as soon as possible.'

'Argentina?'

'Believe me, if you stay here, you'll end up thinking South America wasn't far enough away.'

Kearney averts his gaze to the fretwork edge of the desk, trying to organise his thoughts. South America.

'I can give you some money, enough to cover your ticket and living expenses for a couple of weeks. Have you …?'

'Yes, I have some savings.'

'I'll send you money on the strength of what's in your account.'

Kearney nods. In other words, a loan.

'Liverpool, so – you'll get a cargo ship from there. Hugo's contact details and the money are in the envelope on the desk.'

'When?' Kearney asks, reaching for the envelope.

'Go in the clothes you're standing up in. Buckley will drive you to Dublin Port.'

'I have some personal things in Camp.'

'Leave them – I'll arrange for Buckley to collect them.'

'This is it, so?'

'A killing too much. Did you ever think you'd see the day?'

'After all I've done for them.'

'It isn't forgotten – if it were, you wouldn't have been given this opportunity.'

'I see.'

'Look, in a year's time, who knows? I'll keep you up to date, don't worry.'

'I didn't serve my country, Sir, to end up becoming an exile.'

'It won't be forever.' The senior officer stands up. 'Let's get you on your way while there's time, eh?'

Desertion, he thinks. Encouraged desertion. He'd shot and had people shot for doing less.

Breege

Something about the man outside the station troubled me. Perhaps it was his impatience, his hard glance at his watch, the sharp look he gave me, like I was a face he once knew, one that had let him down. A dapper man with an edge to him.

When we got home, I'd mentioned him to Wilson and he said he was a severe-looking fella, most likely from the ranks of people who resented being kept waiting but who didn't mind delaying others. He was a soldier, most likely an officer – that was easy suss when we saw the army motor passing us for the station.

It had been a good day – the boys' first visit to the city, their second time on a train. Sprouting up, they are; under my nose last year, almost as tall as me now.

I had marked Chalky's height against the side of a bedroom door – the Anto lad is a half-inch taller than his brother was at the same age.

Chalky would have been twenty in January. A year murdered.

Wilson, whose feet have been itching him for an hour, says, 'I'm off to Harte's for a couple for pints.'

'You'll be down later,' I say.

'I wasn't planning to,' he says.

'Perhaps you should plan to,' I say, half-smiling.

'I will, so. I'll stick to the one pint.'

'Good. You're not much use to a woman with a belly full of porter in you.'

Off whistling he goes, like a cat in anticipation of cream.

I close the door after him, secure the bolts top and bottom, and sit by the fire. The boys have had their supper and have gone to bed to read their new books. It had been a fierce early start for them this morning and they're worn out.

It doesn't get any easier, the missing. Not having a grave to visit. They say next year, sometime in 1924. The Committee are striving for a date in early spring.

I don't bother attending the meetings any more. Not since the falling out with Mrs J and a couple of the women who said they were proud that their sons had died for Ireland and would offer them up again for the cause. As if giving birth to their sons entitled them to a say in how they died, or indeed managed their lives even after they'd reached a certain age.

No, Jesus, I couldn't listen to that sort of shite. I said so – I said, 'Listen here, youse – I'd sooner have a live coward on my hands than a dead hero.'

Astonished, they were.

'What did their dying achieve? Nothing – we still have twenty-six counties. Collins won out.'

No life is worth any cause. De Valera kept himself

out of a box in 1916 when he informed the authorities that he was an American citizen. Cute hoor all right. Stood by and watched his colleagues take their bullets. No way was he a martyr. All he's good for, that fella, is lording it over the graves of fallen young fellas, saying what great lads they were for dying. He'll live a long life, that lad, bad cess to him.

Poor Sean McKinley, who kissed my hand outside a dance one night, died from a long illness three days ago. I heard he had wasted to nothing, God love him. He was an officer in the National Army, as they call themselves, and such pomp – they had a military band marching at the front of the gun carriage, five priests met him at the parish church, a bugler played the Last Post at his graveside and ten soldiers fired volleys of shots over his grave, startling many in the large attendance. Mrs Fleming said she'd wet her knickers with the fright. A big send-off – you'd think Sean had died in battle or doing some noble and heroic act of self-sacrifice. He did nothing, only die at home in his bed. His widow, Mary, made out that he'd never fully recovered from being shot in the forearm two years ago. Perhaps there's truth in this.

Eileen wants us all down in Courtown for the summer, maintains that shock triggers off all manner of problems in the human constitution.

I love the heat of the fire in my face.

Ah, here he is – I knew he wouldn't stay away long. He'd be afraid that the cream would curdle. No fear. The knock is his. Three slight raps on the door.

'It's me,' he whispers.

'It better be you or some other fella's in for a grand old time of it.'

The leaves are back on the trees and the weather is mild and airy.

Wilson is helping George in his shop in Naas for a couple of weeks, to learn all about the drapery business, the bookkeeping side of things in particular. I think he has an idea of going into the business – men's fashion. I suppose it'll keep the lads togged out in reasonable clothing, better than the market does – the selection from dead men's bins and racks doesn't be the best. It's been a morning scrubbing clothes on the decker and putting them through the ringer. The boys went off the morning with a crowd of fellas to the woods on Silliot Hill. I thought about holding them back, but Anto begged me to let them go – they were going to play Hide-go-Seek.

'And smoke,' I said.

'I promise we won't.'

When someone makes you a promise, it's best to let him off, to learn for himself how hard a promise can be to keep.

The meeting. Not just any meeting, but an extraordinary meeting, which can only mean one thing: Chalky and the others are coming home.

Now and then I sense his presence in the cottage. When I told Wilson this, he said that he'd often wondered where the smell of Woodbine cigarette smoke was coming from and had put it down to a visitor or that I'd had Chalky's clothes in the kitchen, out to replace the mothballs.

'Or that you yourself were enjoying the odd smoke,' he said.

'I'm not.'

'Then to tell you the truth, I can't figure out the source of the smell.'

The Committee is seated behind tables in the lounge of Harte's Hotel. I order a small glass of porter and sit near the double doors with the frosted glass, on a chair old Paddy Clancy got up off to let me have, saying his legs and back couldn't tolerate the sitting down. I see a few of the other parents. A couple acknowledge my presence, the others don't.

We look through each other.

A spindly looking middle-aged man rises to his feet and calls the house to order. When he achieves a fairish semblance of this, he says, 'Ladies and gentlemen, we have good news for you, at long last.'

The good news is that the boys are coming home. Permission has been granted for the bodies to be exhumed from the Glasshouse yard. Reinterment will take place at the Grey Abbey cemetery in a week's time. This day next week, in fact.

Two hundred yards across from our backyard – amongst the ruins of the Franciscan abbey, burned out by Henry VIII. All that's left is a shell of a building, humps of grass to suggest where the Earls of Kildare are buried, hollows and dips to announce the foundation of a wall here and there – buried amongst princes and rogues and National Army officers.

'There are, however, some preconditions we must honour.'

And in his fall into silence, we strain our ears so as not to drop a word when he resumes speaking.

'There are to be no military trappings of any sort, no flags, no band, no bugler. Nothing, including no gun salute.'

Sighs and mutterings and curses breathed out loud – who the fuck do they think they are? Bastards, sons of bad bitches. No way!

The solicitor lets them talk themselves out, his hands trying to wave them into silence.

When the racket ebbs enough for him to continue, he says, 'This is how it is. If we don't accept their terms, no exhumation will be allowed.'

They don't want to see that it is the winners who dictate the terms. Finally, it is agreed upon via a show of hands. No military ceremony. He looks down at a woman to his right and nods for her to record the details in the minutes book.

'Next,' he says, 'location …'

He tells us that the parish priest, Father Peter Swan, had declined permission for use of his church for the occasion.

Again. Uproar.

Why? Surely this couldn't have come as a surprise to them? This is common practice. Most priests preach against the conflict and had come out in support of the National Army – many priests refused to hear a republican's confession unless he signed a form accepting the Treaty.

I need to visit the toilet. Bursting. Porter just runs through me, but I had to have something in my hand for the sake of giving it something to do.

'I have made all the relevant enquiries – Kildare Courthouse will be made available to us.'

Across from the post office, next to the butt of a tower that used to form part of a Geraldine castle in medieval times, the keep still standing.

Sights familiar to Chalky.

From the floor a woman shouts, 'The lads wouldn't want to be in his bloody church.'

Applause.

Well, it's true – they wouldn't. And whatever else there is to say about Father Swan, it cannot be truth-fully said that he is a hypocrite.

He talks through some other details: date, timings, asks that if any next of kin wishes to arrange a sepa-rate funeral for their loved one to let him know in pri-vate when the meeting is over.

My thoughts on this are hazy. It would not look right for him to be lying apart from them in the ceme-tery. I don't think it is what he would want.

Does it matter? Can you walk into the cemetery and locate a grave of one of the earls? Just one. No. They're dead four centuries – and it's the same for us all. Time wipes us out.

Still, part of me does not like the idea of seeing him in a plot other than his family's, other than with his father. But on the other hand, the smell of cigarette smoke when there is no explanation for it and the noise of a book falling onto the bedroom floor inclines me to think that the grave does not contain us.

A week later, the engine of the lorry cuts out in the yard at the back of the courthouse, beside the keep, and the bearer parties set to work.

View the remains? One of the mothers had asked an hour ago.

Her husband said, 'Ah, no, no, it wouldn't be right and he would prefer you to have a better last memory of him. He's dead too long for the viewing.'

It is wet and rainy. Dark. The bearer parties shoulder the coffins from the bed of the truck and carry them to the front door, stepping off with the inside foot so as to lessen the rocking of the coffins on their shoulders.

One by one to the front of the temporary church – we stand behind Chalky's coffin, me and Wilson and my two boys. I touch the wood where his head touches and I fill up and whisper his name and in the throw of blessed water by the priest I catch my son's tears on my cheek.

There is an aisle flanked by railings of candles and seats either side. The railings lead to four plain wooden coffins and three more ahead of these. They are dressed across the centre with white linen clothes bearing the motif of a red cross. Bouquets of flowers and large cards hold the name in large bold print and with RIP underneath. How can I be sure that it is my son in the coffin bearing his name?

I can't be. That he is one of them is all I can be certain of.

The padre is a forceful speaker and perhaps as much outside the realm of his church as we are, but he is a priest – or at least he wears the vestments of one. A good crowd has gathered, many not from the town – but then, we had expected this would happen. The rift is wide and we'll all be dead a long time before there's a joining.

After the Mass, we file slowly past the coffins and pay our respects, shake the hands of those who want to offer us their condolences. In Harte's Hotel, drink and sandwiches have been laid on, a bit of a sing-song arranged to see the lads off. For they didn't hear a song in their ears since the night before Moore's Bridge …

But I stay here, in the courthouse, along with the other parents, to keep the souls company, leaving Wilson and Sheila to tend to the boys.

This is a vigil I have been waiting for.

I think of him, the moment he was born, his first cry, holding him in my arms, seeing him take his first few steps, the way he would cling to me when a wind turned a certain way in the middle of the night – growing up, growing away from me, but still the bond remained – and the pain I feel at the loss of him will never lessen.

In the middle of the night, Wilson brings me a mug of tea laced with sugar and a little brandy in it to sweeten my skin against the cold. In this temporary

church, in the candlelight, there's a peace and a serenity that I could hold onto forever.

But nothing lasts.

'Are you okay?' Wilson asks, sitting beside me after
whispering his condolences to Mrs J and Mrs Mangan
and her husband, the women in black and black hats
– me too. I hate the colour, the trussed-up feel. But it
is a matter of respect.

I nod.

'Good. The boys are in bed,' he says.

His presence is slightly irritating. Stupid questions.
Am I okay? To look at me, one would instantly know
that I was far from being okay.

'You can go on, Wilson, get some sleep.'

'I'm grand,' he says.

He takes out his rosary beads and looks straight
ahead at the coffins, blesses himself.

I reach out and hold his hand. Squeeze.

The next morning, the crowd is so large that not all can fit inside the courthouse. I find it difficult to breathe in the cramped space. My undergarments are stuck to me with the sweat. The tip of my finger is numb, has been since the other day when I carried home a heavy bag of messages – I think the thin rope handles trapped a nerve. I notice too, of late, that the corner of my upper lip twitches. Obviously these are signs, like storm clouds in the offing. Wilson maintains it is the culmination of the last two years exacting its toll, that I'll be fine by the summer. I was a summer soul, he said, and needed the sun on my back. I had to laugh – did he think I was a horse?

I worry about not being around for Anto and Seanie. Though my being around did not stop this awful fate befalling my eldest.

There is a mixture of bad odours. Raindrops tick against the long, narrow windows. Fresh air sweeps in when a side-door opens and chases the swoon from me. Great, welcoming blasts of rainy air. Candle flames bend in the breeze and straighten again in its absence.

And so the cortege moves in solemn procession to the old cemetery. By the hospital, the nunnery, the parish church, passing by our home a hundred yards away, down the Tully road, on to Grey Abbey, through the black iron gates.

Civic police and plainclothes detectives look on. I glance at them, impervious men, geared for trouble, hoping for a reason to start wielding their truncheons, loosening their revolvers, letting us know by their volume in numbers that they are in charge. Enjoying the spectacle.

Go away and let us bury our dead in peace, why don't ye? Haunting them to the grave – what sort are ye? Murderers.

Pushing and shoving.

There is no room for the police near the mass grave. We mourners are tightly pressed together, black umbrellas raised against the milling rain. The skies are black – all is black. Hammering noise of the rain on the umbrellas, on old headstones, swelling on the underbelly of branches before falling onto the thick hummocks of raw earth stolen from the ground for as long as it takes to lower seven coffins. The priest shouts about the bloodletting, the bloodstained earth of our brethren, the true Sons of Erin who refused to bend the knee to the English, who did not abandon their Northern brethren, who paid the ultimate sacrifice.

'May God diffuse their spirit among us.'

I look at my boys either side of me and I see their pale complexions and how the priest's words buff their pride, bring up their anger. No tears from them, and I sense that though they watch the proceedings with great interest, they still remain a little detached. Is this a good thing?

They begin to lower the coffins.

Hail Mary … Our Father …

I see the revolver being produced and the curled finger on the trigger. In quick succession, three shots break the air. A cloud of smoke lingers, its smell like smoked powder. The police move in, wedging into the crowd. Much jostling and pushing and shoving and cursing. An old woman is knocked to the ground and is helped up, only for the people assisting her to be driven on top of her. All fall down.

Appeals for calm.

The first spills of shovelled clay onto the coffins, mayhem amidst the priest's final prayers. I take hold of my two boys and push them ahead of me to the south, through a gap that appeared when several men of a bearer party broke for a boundary wall, the police giving chase. We stop and turn about at the abbey ruins and wait there and look back and watch the mêlée and Wilson running about looking for us, spotting us then and running towards us, dodging a policeman's reach for him.

God, the alarm on his face for the moments he couldn't find us makes me think.

The men are searched as they leave the cemetery, measured against the low dry stone walls and patted down. But they don't search the women for some reason. And if they had done this, they would have found the revolver in a closed umbrella.

Wilson and I and the boys walk home. Motors pass us by, the graveyard emptying. I will return later on my own to talk a while with Chalky.

A month later, I come to see the lie of things. The hatred on both sides is deep. I don't want to live in this town with two boys who have acquired a none-too-valuable legacy: a brother viewed by one side as a martyr and the other as a brigand.

The other evening, I overheard Anto saying to Seanie, 'When I'm old enough, I'm going to join the Irregulars and fight for Ireland like Chalky.'

Seanie says, 'Yeah, yeah, me too.'

'We'll practise with the hurleys in the woods until we get real guns.'

'What about Mammy?'

'She has Wilson.'

I remained very calm and went downstairs and pulled out a drawer in the dresser and took out their dead brother's unopened letters and brought them up and handed them over.

'Read these. I haven't read them – I think he may have some solid advice for youse.'

Not for one whit did the advice matter. The next day they were off across the fields with hurleys resting on their shoulders. Without doubt, their brother's brothers.

Six weeks to the day the lads were laid to rest in Grey Abbey, Wilson sits me down at the kitchen table and pours me a brandy.

'I'm not over fond of that stuff,' I say.

'It'll coax the bitterness and the disappointment out of you.'

I look at him as he hands me the glass. God love him, but there's not a pick of flesh on his bones. There's the want of a hundred good dinners in him. A poor set of teeth to him, too – me thinking this and I owning a fair collection of bad ones myself.

He smokes. I don't.

'Drink up,' he says.

I suppose it's poison in to take worse poison out.

We talk about this and that. His dead brother. George and his unhappy marriage. How much it hurt him to see me hurting. He stops talking and I tell him what I'd heard and seen the boys saying and doing. He sighs and shrugs as though to say there's feck all can be done about it.

He says, 'If you don't want the boys to play with a ball, you take away the ball or get them off the pitch.'

'Ah, don't do Jesus Christ – God forgive me for using his name – and be talking in parables.'

'You know what I'm on about.'

I sip at the brandy. 'You watch,' I say, 'who does well out of the war.'

And Wilson, droll as a stuffed parrot, says, 'There'll be a few who'll build rotten empires on bad money.'

'How can my boys ever forget if I don't distance them from this town of arse-lickers and fucking weasel heads? They think I don't know – I know all right, Wilson. Young Wogan Browne – who did what with the stolen money? Ah, stand by sure and watch – watch a man come from nothing and open a business and ask yourself where he got the capital. They're all grabbing what they can – republicans and the provisional government in the void left by the British. There'll be jobs for this lad because his daddy fought on this or that side. Jobs for this one because her mother passed on vital information.'

'We don't have to stand by and watch,' he says.

Away from this place. With its proud history of Brigid and Viking-age round tower and its stony streets full of fearful hearts. They won't talk openly of this incident in town for many a year – people will walk around afraid to mention the war, the crimes perpetrated, the blood spilled, afraid because people who murdered walk free with impunity, an informer lives, perhaps two. And my son and most of those who died with him died for being caught in possession of weapons. To shoot dead three young men: two of eighteen and another of nineteen was an act of barbarity. They killed no one, put no gun to a British officer's head and shot him dead. And four men guilty of identical offences in Kerry, in possession of weapons, received the death penalty but had their sentences rescinded. What's the differ? No one will ever tell me.

The man who pulled the trigger that killed the officer that morning is alive and well. The other man who done in Thos Behan and killed Bergin is on the run.

He'll be caught, I hope. If life isn't fair, then life during wartime is less so.

'I've been doing a lot of thinking, Wilson.'

He says very quietly, 'What is it you'd like to do, Breege?'

'There is Eileen's offer of a move to Courtown, but I'm inclined to think that the island is too small for us to start afresh with a new identity, a new life.'

'Canada,' he says, 'or the States?'

When I suddenly remember Chalky reading a piece to me from a journal, about the remnant Irish battalions of the American Civil War invading Canada, I say, 'Canada – would that suit you better?'

'It would.'

I nod.

'Breege, you're sure?'

'Yes. Let's do this, Wilson.'

This is the right move for the boys, I am sure of it. Above all my fears, my dislike at the prospect of change, of leaving Chalky behind, the upheaval.

I am sure. When we're leaving, I won't look back.

'So …?'

'So, Wilson?'

'Does this mean you'll marry me?'

'We've had everything else, we may as well have the cake.'

He comes over and takes my hand and draws me up to him. I know what he's going to say and I put my fingers to his lips and seal the words and say, 'The last time a man promised he wouldn't give me reason to regret it, well, he did. No promises, Wilson, just do your best and I'll do mine.'

247

Epilogue

1929

Vancouver is cold and sunny this morning. Bright autumn sunshine – the fall, they call it here. Fall, an appropriate word when I think on it, the fall of leaves, the fall in temperature. Change before renewal – life's cycle. Wilson is fond of saying that we see the resurrection take place every spring. He doesn't like it very much when I tell him he's spending too much time with his friends from the Philosophical Society, who, of course, meet in the pub. I love the city life, have taken to it much better than I had expected. It felt strange to remove my wedding ring, such an effort I had, soap and water and in the end it had to be cut by a jeweller, a Jewish man called Gross.

Wilson's ring, it's easy to admit, is a far more comfortable fit.

Eileen arrived on a holiday. I hadn't seen her since my wedding five years ago. She left ten days ago to spend some time with her sister-in-law in New Orleans. She left behind a padded brown envelope containing newspapers that had articles in them she had thought I might be interested in. She went to the trouble of Xing them with Biro for me. I delayed reading them till now. What was the hurry? None. I had considered leaving them unread, but curiosity got the better of me. I waited for the time to be right before laying my eyes on the words, and I have no idea why the right time is now, only that it is.

I remove these pieces of news from the envelope and spread them on the table. I put on my spectacles, the half-moon type, which I think makes me too matronly looking. The boys laughed when they first saw me wearing them – afterwards they said I wasn't squinting any more. I had gone fierce bad for squinting. I read from *The Kildare Observer.*

'Bergin's murder was only one of a nearly hundred during the Civil War. He was slain as a beast would be slain. Many others were done to death in the same terrible way. In many cases, as apparently in Bergin's, the victims were first tortured and then killed, usually because they would not betray their fellows.'

Hmm. Newspapers give you the gist of things, I think, not the full story.

I think some people don't need a reason to torture and kill people, they do it because they enjoy doing it.

The next paper.

'Former Captain Arthur Kearney, returned from the Argentine after being persuaded to come back for a normal jury trial. He is an ex-Army intelligence officer. Kearney insisted during the trial that he was a scapegoat in the murder. James Cleary, a soldier, in evidence for the prosecution, stated that on 13 December 1922, Colonel Conor Costello, Director of

Intelligence, had ordered him to give a car to Captain Kearney. When the car was returned to him the following day, "it was covered in blood in the inside". Three days later, Pte Cleary was detained and held in Arbour Hill Prison for four months and was never told on what charge he was held. Lt Col Conor Costello stated, "Corporal Bergin was in illicit communications with the Irregulars and republican prisoners in Tintown Internment Camp – I sent Captain Kearney to investigate the report." It emerged during the course of the trial that Col Costello assisted Captain Kearney in leaving the jurisdiction.'

Another paper, a different date.

'A former National Army officer, Captain Arthur Kearney, was yesterday found guilty in Dublin District Court of the murder of Cpl Joseph Bergin. He was sentenced to death on June 12, but his sentence was later commuted to life imprisonment. A former Lieutenant, Joe Buckley, and Sergeant Anthony Higgins, both charged with the murder of Corporal Bergin, had their charges dropped.'

A mercy shown to Kearney that he did not show to others. Only the leader carries the buck – another mercy doled out to Buckley and Higgins. God, the country must be changing entirely – there was a time not so long ago that they shot king and serf. Buckley and Higgins swung their colleague out to dry.

The last newspaper, a few lines reporting the death of ex-Captain Arthur Kearney, who had been serving a life sentence in Maryborough Prison. 'Witnesses to the prisoner taking his own life were two prison warders, one of whom, Eddie Hennigan, stated, 'Mr Kearney jumped from the landing on the upper stairwell.' It had been reported that Mr Kearney had been in negotiations with a prominent national newspaper concerning a sensational story he wanted to tell. The editor of the said newspaper stated that the story was "fanciful, and one not worthy of publication."'

The name Hennigan is familiar to me …

There is more: a cutting concerning the assassination of the Minister of Justice in 1927 after he'd attended a football game – why did she include this? Was he a signature that had sent the lads to their end? Was it not Cosgrave?

I glance at the clock. *Is that the time? Jesus, I better get the dinner on.* They'll be in soon with hanging tongues, asking what's for dinner – Shepherd's Pie Day, Anto had said this morning, licking his lips and he just after eating breakfast.

Just as I am about to rise, little Steve barges in through the back door, asking me if the boys are home. He is snotty-nosed and beautiful. Stocky. His daddy's darling. Mine, too. He wants to know when the boys are coming home from school – he has no one to play with.

'I'm here, amn't I?' I say, putting my arms round him, patting down his sticky-up hair with a finger of spittle.

'Will you play Cowboys and Indians with me?'

'Sure, but only for a few minutes. I have to start dinner.'

He takes me by the hand, hurrying us outside to the long, wide backyard. The grass is long, the log piles neatly stacked, an axe buried in a tree stump, the wooden fencing half-creosoted, a task Wilson had set for the boys if they want pocket money. He's full of modern notions, that lad. It's him that has the boys in college and not working. Education, education, he says.

Steve lets go of my hand and runs to a timber shed behind a pair of sycamores. He stoops to pick up his toy bow and arrow and his plastic tomahawk where he had dropped them when he grew bored and teary. Up to this very moment I didn't think there was much of a resemblance between him and his half-brother. For moments, in the diffused light of the bony canopy and the cant of his head to indicate that we can begin playing, I see my oldest son in him. The likeness is stark and somewhat uncanny – and then the ghost fades.

A Note from the Author

While *The Silence of the Glasshouse* is a work of fiction, it is rooted in historical fact. Lieutenant John Wogan Browne was murdered in Kildare Town in February 1922. In December of that year seven anti-treaty troops were executed in the largest official execution ordered by an Irish government, ostensibly for being found in unlawful possession of arms and ammunition. The same week four volunteers who were arrested in Kerry for a similar crime had their death sentences rescinded. The remains of the executed Kildaremen were interred in the Glasshouse and exhumed in 1924 for burial at Grey Abbey.

Much of the historical information for this book was gleaned from articles written by historians Mario Corrigan, James Durney and Adrian Mullowney. Others passed on local oral traditions, for which I thank them. I also thank The Arts Council who awarded me a literary bursary that enabled me to complete this book. It should be noted that *The Silence of the Glasshouse* is based on my radio play, *Song of the Small Bird*, broadcast by RTÉ Drama and produced by Aidan Mathews.